THE MIND'S ASPIRATION

A SHORT STORY COLLECTION

T J BAINZ

CONTENTS

A SILENT COMPANY

H ANDS CLASPED.
        Hearts beating.

A hard, terrible silence drifts down, settles upon the room.

The first hours of the winter sun bleed in through white, netted curtains, illuminating the pitifully mediocre hotel room.

Its light illuminates the furniture: the twin beds, shifted a shoulder's width apart; the bedside tables, a well-worn, cheap imitation pinewood; the faded dirty-green carpets, once, surely, the exact shade of the verdant bushes which grow thickly beyond the windows of the hotel.

The dead television screen reflects the illuminated windows, shines them back like an encore into the rest of the room.

A smell of furniture polish and damp clings to the place. Even if it was warm enough to latch open the windows all the way, it would be doubtful that this particular measure alone would rid the room of the dual odours.

When Hillary turns on her side, she hears the slight slinking sound of the white sheets against her skin. She can *feel* the dry washing powder which sticks to the material. She can still taste the milk from the room-service cereal they ordered not ten minutes ago, and the bowls of which—the emptied cardboard packaging— lie over on the desktop, scattered beside the television like a pair of afterthoughts in the otherwise orderly room.

It was never meant to end like this.

Not here.

Not now.

Hillary can hear his breathing. The gentle rise and fall of his chest. She recalls how, back when they first met, she would often wake in the middle of the night, caffeine still pumping through her veins, and simply listen to his respiration. It would calm her—have

3

some sort of a soothing effect over her, and, eventually, though far from instantaneously, she would slip back under sleep's spell.

Now, though, it only served to keep her on edge.

To keep her on her toes.

Every muscle in her body seized tight, and she could hear her heart beating against her throat. And her mind scrambling to stay sharp, if required at a moment's notice.

Hillary shifts her weight a little. The bed creaks. Her heart beats a few hard little pulses, sends the blood welling in her veins. She wants, more than anything else, to escape this place. To be anywhere else than here. But, at the same time, she knows she cannot leave. That, though it appears so simple in theory, that she could just shuck the bed sheet, pull on her dress and leave the room, in reality it's an impossibility.

Those dozen or so steps are just too far.

Too long of a journey to make.

Because there shall be no turning back.

And so she just lies there—*still*.

Outside, she can hear car engines starting up in the car park. People leaving the wedding. Those who stayed overnight. Just stirring. Their hangovers from the hotel reception the night before very much intact. Ready to slog their way back home. To drive whichever roads they must drive to reach their destination.

Hillary wishes she had somewhere to head home to.

Somewhere *different* to go.

But she has only here.

And she has only *now*.

Future has gone.

Past has gone.

What remains?

In the end, it's him who makes the first move.

Hillary turns slightly to watch. Keeping her face almost hidden behind the bed sheets.

She doesn't want him to know she's watching.

Just like she has teased him about a million times, he makes a great furore of shifting out from beneath his covers, jettisoning them onto the floor, in a pile.

Naked, he steps across the hotel room carpet, not bothering with the flip-flops she constantly chides him to use whenever walking about indoors.

He brings the toilet door shut with a *whompf* of escaping air.

And Hillary is alone again.

In bed.

On her own.

And she knows—now, more than ever—that this is the time to leave.

To slip away.

~

Hillary only has time to catch herself—for her rational mind to click into play—when she reaches the bottom of the staircase, in the hotel reception. She stands there briefly. She blinks in the harsh, *bright* white winter's daylight which dribbles in through the windows. Although she wishes to hold up her forearm, to shield herself from the brightness, she does nothing of the sort.

She smiles at the grey-suited, blond kid on reception. He has the whitest teeth she has ever seen, and appears to have manicured nails too. She wonders when men stopped being men, when everything got so blurry that nothing could ever be made out—*distinguished*—any longer.

Her heels clack against the well-polished floor of the reception, and she can feel her heart pounding. Already, within her own mind, she documents her imagined movements of him, back up in the hotel room.

Has he yet emerged from the bathroom?

Has he peered about the room?

Noticed that she has gone?

Or is he still oblivious?

Does he think things are just the way they are?

The way they *were?*

The way they shall *always* be?

Once outside, her mind clears, and she can see straight once again.

She can see the space stretching out before the tip of her nose.

The world once more spins into being.

This whole sorry *thing* shall be left behind.

As if she anticipated these feelings, Hillary parked her car up on the other side of the hotel car park. The perfect spot for her getaway. She has only to drive off. To leave all of this behind. And she shall be safe, once again.

But isn't safety only relative?

Won't she, in truth, merely be barrelling along into the next circumstance?

Eyes closed?

The *scrub* of the key in the driver's door of her tiny, scarlet-red hatchback sends a shudder passing over the surface of her skin. Perhaps she was worse for wear the night before. Worse off than she thought. She's never been that good of a judge of her limits— either of what she *can* do, or what she *can't.*

Only when she sits behind the wheel does she feel safe.

She grips the rutted plastic tightly.

Breathes in deeply.

And out again.

She peers through the windscreen, to the car park.

And she sees her.

His sister.

Hillary takes her in. Absorbs her appearance. The dumpy cheeks—the *dumpier* frame—and how his sister, even in a light, casual, baggy t-shirt and jeans, looks overweight. She looks bitter about her situation, about how the world sees her.

About how Hillary *sees* her.

No amount of eye makeup can mask that.

Their eyes cross.

Hillary's heart pounds.

She feels a cold sweat break out over the surface of her skin.

But she needs to go.

She needs to go *now*.

Too late.

The sister, she approaches.

Hillary scrabbles for her keys. Just in time she slots them into the ignition. But it's too late. Already it's too late. The sister stands up at her window. She glares in like a wronged pensioner. Her eyes mean, and questioning, and searing through skin.

With a soft motion, she raps her knuckles against the glass.

Hillary holds still. She finds herself caught between two eventualities.

Drive off, leave this all behind.

Or, stop, wait, speak with the sister.

See what she wants.

Hillary knows not which action to take.

And so fate decides for her.

It visits itself upon her.

Hillary's hand reaches out for the button on the armrest. With an electronic *purr* the window winds itself down, into nothing. The cold, crispy air creeps into the car. Hillary longs to start the engine, and to click the heaters on. To breathe some life into her bones.

The sister regards Hillary for long moments—*impossibly long moments.*

Then she parts her lips, those *piggy* lips of hers, and she says, "Creeping out, are we?"

Hillary looks back at the sister. She tries to keep her throat from constricting. She feels a flourish of blood to the head. But she keeps herself level. She is an adult, and as such must act like one. She must be responsible for her actions.

She must meet them head on . . . and *connect* with the outside world.

"I'm leaving," Hillary replies, finally.

The sister gives a slight nod. She parts her lips. "Don't suppose anybody's spoken with you, have they?"

Hillary shakes her head. Then her gaze somehow slips from the sister's, and she finds herself looking on out from beneath the glass of the windscreen. Out to the façade of the hotel. She can see him there. Dressed in his suit from the night before. Perhaps the first thing that he managed to get his hands on.

Hillary glances back to the sister. "Nobody's spoken to me," she says.

"Just as well," the sister replies, "Don't think they'll have nothing nice to say."

Hillary sees that *he* sees her. And that he advances towards her. That he weaves his way through the parked cars. He holds himself upright, straight-backed, that way which, she supposes, he was either taught, or taught himself to do. He looks ragged and unkempt in his suit, all flustered. He needs to shave urgently, but hasn't had time given the circumstances. When he approaches, the sister seems to anticipate him, and she turns around. Flashes her eyebrows to him. The two of them exchange a glance. With a nod, the sister sweeps off away from the side of the car.

She never looks back to Hillary.

Hillary feels the sister slip out of her life.

Gone forever.

Thank God.

He stands before her now, though.

Hillary's fingers rest on the car keys. She knows just a gentle motion will be all it will take. And then she can set the car purring. Drive herself away from here.

In the distance, the blurred figures carry their suits and dresses in plastic cases.

Keeping them pristine.

Keeping them from damage.

To look at *him*, standing here, before her, is almost to picture the living dead.

Crawled up out from the grave.

From the cold death of the night before.

"You're going?" he says, his voice level, emotionless.

Hillary nods yes.

He breaks their gaze. He glances about the car.

Is he looking for *their* car?

Seeing if she's *still* there?

Hillary knows that she left long ago. Hillary heard the stirring of a car engine early in the morning, soon after he had shifted his weight off her, laid himself down beside her, that sickly, drunken grin on his lips.

If he asks Hillary for a ride to the station then she will deny him.

This is where it ends.

This is where it ends for *them*.

He reaches up and scratches the back of his neck. It makes a sound that Hillary cannot stand. She pictures the skin flaking off beneath his fingernails. She ceases thinking about it.

No longer able to bear the mental image.

"So," she says, "I'm sorry for ruining your life."

Against all odds, he gives a slight—*wry*—smile. His eyes swivel a little in their sockets, in a still-drunk, dopey way. He gives a shrug. "All it needed was a little push—just one little nudge for it to go tumbling over the cliff."

"And I was that nudge?" Hillary says.

He nods back at her.

Hillary breathes in deep. She wonders if she can escape here without too many injuries. She has had enough of getting hurt. Of her life being out in the public domain. Of living as she did the night before, in glare, and scandal, and *hate*.

She wants to disappear.

She reaches for the keys in the ignition, feels the gentle weight of the mechanism, all ready for her to turn. And to leave this place blazing. In her wake. Nothing more than a fragmented memory in her rear-view mirror.

But he scuppers all those hopes. He reaches out, lays his hands down on the open window of the car. He bends into the car. His eyes meet hers for a long time, and Hillary can smell the stale beer on his breath, mingled with red wine, or whatever else it was that he was supping on the sly. She wonders if he might kiss her. That really would be the frosting on the cake for anybody observing the scene.

Hillary wonders if anybody might be watching from the hotel windows, sneaking a peek at this unfolding drama out in the car park. She wonders if there aren't some guests from the wedding who couldn't sleep last night for the excitement. As if they might be about to witness a blockbuster presentation . . . and all through their own eyes.

And their own frame of reference.

"I won't forget," he says to her, still bent over, his hands still lying on the window ledge.

"No," Hillary says, "I suppose you won't."

He remains in the same position for the longest time, for so long that Hillary believes she will never escape. She can still feel the hundred invisible eyes of the hotel all glaring down on her —*judging* her.

What do they *want* from her?

What do they *expect* from her?

There'll be no winding back the clocks, and, anyway, it takes two to tango.

Two to wield the hammer.

In such silent company.

He holds himself there, blocking the pathway forwards in her life, and Hillary wills him away. But he stays in that place. She knows that she will have to be the one to say. The one who shall, once and for all, put a stop to any hope, or any desire.

Feeling herself welling up, but keeping the tears from quite rising to the surface, she looks into his eyes, finds herself—just like the night before—getting lost within them. Getting lost within *him*. And she finds the hatred—the *self*-hatred—rising within her chest.

Becoming so palpable that it might as well be a balloon, fit to burst.

"I'm going," she says, this time her voice unable to rise above a whisper.

He seems to track her weakness.

He extends a finger—nothing *more*—and he reaches out to her.

Strokes her cheek.

Hillary feels that same shudder pass through her. She feels it lock hold of her bones. Rattle them about within her skin. She wants to pull away, and yet she knows that she cannot. That although his touch brings back all the horrible, it also brings back the wonder, and the fantasy, and the pleasure. And it will take more strength than she can reasonably expect to wield in order to resist.

Strength which she finds within herself.

She draws away from him.

His fingers slip through the air.

Retreat back to his side.

He stands there, lips slightly latched open.

Hillary turns the ignition. She jams her finger down on the

button. Winds the window back upwards. That whining *purr* seems almost like a concerto. What it tells her, Hillary cannot say for certain. But she realises its significance.

That she leaves the past behind that innocuous little sound.

She lets out the handbrake, floors the accelerator.

Ploughs out through the car park.

Past the opened barrier.

And she only dares look back just as she turns the corner, leaving the hotel behind forever. And she sees him standing there, in just the same place as before, stunned, confused—everything which she feels herself.

But she knows she can share nothing.

AN INVENTION HOPEFULLY
NOT TOO LATE FOR ITS TIME

1

HENRIETTA DAVIS tottered her way along the pavement. Her pair of sea-green high heels gave a smart *click* against the cement.

In the road alongside her, cars all stood stuck in a never-ending traffic jam. Bumper to bumper. Knuckles white clasping steering wheels. Slighted glares staring out from under windscreens.

Contamination billowed out from—seemingly—everywhere, though, in reality, Henrietta understood that the majority was spewing forth from the car exhausts.

At the rate Henrietta was going, she had to crane her neck back to take gulps from the virgin air that passed just above her head. Like a goldfish gobbling at the top of its tank. And, even thinking about it now, she was not at all flattered by *that* comparison.

The mint she'd slipped between her lips as she'd come up from the metro station had helped a little. Some people said that sucking on a mint was just like slugging back an espresso. Gave you crisp, clear thinking. Stuff like that.

She begged to differ.

Her calves ached. The soles of her feet ached. The skin on the sides of her toes ached. And she just wanted to get to the meeting. Just wanted to get to the meeting on time.

She was running late. Was at that annoying time. Ten minutes to go. Knew that if she was just to walk quickly she might well make it right on the button.

But she would have to go quickly.

Have to speed right along as fast as she could go in these heels of hers.

Risk sweat soggying her nicely cut, and long-time chosen golden-cream suit jacket over a pair of sensible, black trousers.

Making her blouse underneath resemble a grease-soaked chip packet. The outfit she had changed four . . . or was it five? . . . times over, just trying to get it right, and found herself running late as a consequence.

Why was it, on days like these, bone-crushingly, spleen-burstingly, blood-pressure-poppingly important days like these that she could never managed to flag down a cab?

Had she pissed off some luck fairy, or god, or voodoo *thing*?

Or was it more sinister?

Some days she could almost *swear* that there was someone out there, out there in the Big Bad World, who was just determined to get at her.

For no discernible reason.

She tottered on a little more. Keeping half an eye out for cracks in the concrete slabs beneath her feet. She brought her handbag round to her front. Sleek black leather. Classic. Simple. She brought the zip open with a neat little *zip*, pawed through and located her phone. Spun through the screens. Got to the map. To her GPS coordinates. Her destination marked with a neat, verdant point.

Streaker Fashions.

Next up.

Just . . . oh *shit*!

She zoomed in closer on the map. Doing that bizarre crab-claw motion. Saw that the office was on the other side of the street.

She glanced about. A little panicked now. Heart welling up in her throat.

Squeezing the blood harder up to her temples.

Bringing on a migraine.

She could just tell.

. . . But, *right there*, ten paces off. Something like that. A zebra crossing.

Salvation.

She tottered on. Using her hands to divide the crowds of people: grey-haired old men with beige cardigans, teenage mothers lugging kids along in pushchairs, women like her, all dressed up for business and clearly running hard against a clock.

And they all seemed to be heading in the opposite direction to her.

As if Henrietta was battling her way upstream.

Like a salmon . . . and there she was, getting fish back on the mind again.

She made the zebra crossing. Didn't dare check the time. She only had eyes for the bronze placard on the other side of the street. The bold lettering that she could see, even from here, read *Streaker Fashions*. Her future. It was right there. Just before her. So close that she could reach out and touch it . . . if she'd had rubber arms, and some extremely complicated—and no doubt *heavy*—ratcheting system installed into her bones, and muscles.

Black and white. Black and white.

Blinking amber lights, a little dulled by the sharp, overcast midday skies.

She took a step out onto the zebra crossing.

And another.

Car engines hummed in her ears.

The exhaust fumes tickled her nose.

But she only had eyes, and to an extent: ears, mouth, and nose, for that placard staring her down. From across the street. Only eyes for *Streaker Fashions*.

Right there.

So close . . . just a few steps—

A car horn blared hard.

Stunned Henrietta.

Her shoulders tensed. She dug her fingernails into her palms.

She dropped her handbag. Stumbled. Somehow her heel found a rut in the zebra crossing. And she tumbled down.

Onto the hard, asphalt surface.

And her head struck hard.

And everything went black.

2

LOTS OF BLEEPING brought Henrietta round. She could feel the uneven, scratchy rub of well-washed fabric against her skin. Her mouth tasted stale. And when she breathed out a hard breath, she was certain she could've stunned a cow. When she breathed in, everything smelled of antiseptic. And floor polish.

She really didn't need to open her eyes to know where she was.

In the hospital.

But she did anyway.

She peered about herself. Her vision a little bleary about the edges.

Lots of colours. Soft colours. All blurred together.

Sludge greens. Baby blues. Autumn browns.

Her heart seeming to be coming out of a lull, slowly starting to throb again. To remember what it was supposed to be doing in her body.

She blinked a couple of times. But that didn't help to clear the haze in her mind.

She felt a distant *thrum* at her forehead, not pain exactly, but not a pleasant feeling by any means. She tried to bring her hand up from beneath her covers but found that she didn't have as much control, as much *strength*, as she imagined. And she just decided to leave it be. To trust that whatever was going on with her forehead, she'd just let it play itself out.

Let the doctors—wherever they were—see to that.

They were the experts, after all.

As she lay there, arms down at her sides, nestled beneath those blankets, and feeling the wooziness drift in and out through her ears, she wondered just what she was doing here.

In the hospital.

She stretched her mind. *Tried* to remember.

She had been outside.

In the street.

Walking.

That was right.

But then . . . then . . .

She could picture the map. The map on her phone. That green little blob marking her destination. But *what* had been her destination? Where had she been going to exactly?

It didn't come clear to her.

All she saw, when she put her mind to it, was black and white, painted onto asphalt.

In the near distance, she could hear the *slap* of flat-soled shoes against hard, well-polished floor. She guessed that was the same hard, well-polished floor that surrounded her.

The *sludge* green floor.

She clasped her eyes shut for another few seconds, and when she opened them again, the world around her had cleared up a great deal.

She could see curtains. Drawn back. That baby blue colour.

And she could now make out the autumn brown blankets that tucked her into this hospital bed.

A couple of blinks later, and she could make out the wall washed in beige paint that confronted her. She could make out several marks where, no doubt, crash trolleys had struck it, where disoriented patients had stumbled and left handprints, or where visitors had kicked it out of frustration.

She wondered if she might have a visitor.

Had she had a visitor?

How long had she been here, cooped up in this hospital bed?

She had no way of knowing.

Just as she put these testy questions to herself, she heard a pair of footsteps break off from the distant rush, and could hear them getting closer. Approaching her.

When she looked up, she saw a nurse.

A *male* nurse.

He had on that same baby blue colour, with a pair of plastic, full-body sandals on his feet.

God, how she hated those.

Ugly as all hell.

The nurse had blond hair, and a kind of dusty complexion. Not exactly tanned, but certainly getting there. Maybe he had been on holiday a month or so ago.

Any glow that had once been there had certainly gone.

He gave her a smile. No teeth in it. Just lips. But a smile nonetheless.

Maybe it was the wooziness, or the confusion about just where she was, but Henrietta found herself reciprocating.

Strange, she almost never smiled at strangers.

Though, this guy was a nurse.

"Great to see you've come round," he said.

Finding the nurse becoming a little blurred, Henrietta blinked another couple of times, trying to get him straightened out again.

The nurse reached over her to some machine that she didn't have the strength to glance back and look at. She just caught sight of the billowing shirt sleeve of his scrubs, and the thickety blond hair at the end of the tunnel burrowed beneath his armpit.

His musky smell, mixed in with some honey-scented cologne, was actually a welcome relief to the antiseptic overload from the hospital ward, though she still remembered clearly how many times, while on the metro, she'd done her best to hold her breath so she wouldn't have to breathe in that rancid assortment of body odour and deodorant, and goodness knew what else.

The nurse finished his playing with the machine behind Henrietta's head, and he stood back, cocked his head to one side, sympathetically, and said, "How're you feeling?"

Henrietta's throat felt dry all of a sudden. And she knew, even before she answered him, that her voice would be frail, and reedy. "Uh, a little confused."

He smiled wider. All the wrinkles in his dusty complexion flattening out as he did so. "Yeah, I'm sure you are." He pressed his lips together, glanced at the machine, and then looked back to Henrietta. "We've run an MRI and found no damage. So it's just a concussion you're shaking off. You hit the ground pretty hard, it turns out."

"Oh, really?" Henrietta said, thinking that she sounded like a disorientated grandmother saying that.

Fine, a disorientated grandmother, and she wasn't even thirty yet . . .

He nodded. "So once you shake it off, you'll be fine to go."

Henrietta still felt like she had a stopper in her brain. Like she just couldn't put all the pieces of the puzzle together. What he said, about her hitting the ground. Yes. That made sense. She *could* remember something about that. The black-and-white lines. The asphalt.

The *road*!

That was it!

She had fallen. Just gone and toppled right over. Her heel had found a crack, and the rest was history. She'd banged her head.

But there were still parts that she had to get right in her mind.

Things that she just couldn't recall totally.

The nurse dipped his hand into his pocket. Withdrew some device—a phone?—and checked over the screen. Then he looked at her again with warm, slightly fuzzy, eyes.

Or maybe that was the concussion, or whatever, coming back at her.

"We've got the possessions you had on you at the time of the accident. I can bring them to you now if you like."

Henrietta thought it over. Tried to get *that* concept straight in her mind.

Yes, that was right.

She didn't have her clothes with her.

Or her handbag . . . so, yes, it made sense that the hospital would've taken them in.

Perfect sense.

She gave him a nod and, with a parting smile, the nurse slipped back off, away from her bedside, and she listened to his footsteps —made by those hideous sandals of his—slip away.

He returned in about five minutes or so, at least it *felt* like five minutes to her. She guessed that she would have to keep an eye on herself, try her best to keep her thoughts straight if she was to have a chance of getting out of here today.

The nurse laid her sleek, black leather handbag down on her lap.

Henrietta thought of telling him that she wasn't strong enough to reach out for it herself, but decided against it. Decided to try and see for herself.

So, under the watchful eye of the nurse, she slowly managed to bring her arms up from her sides, and out from beneath the covers. This wasn't so hard after all. It was just a matter of practice really.

Just a mental block.

Though her fingertips felt numb, she managed to bring the handbag closer. To reach for the zip, and holding the handbag firm with her other hand, to latch the zip back and to bring it open. As she stared into the blackness within, a faint sense a familiarity now sweeping over her, the nurse spoke.

"We tried to find someone close to you—someone to call and let them know that you were here, but we couldn't manage to get through to anyone on your phone." The nurse pressed his lips together. "Well, what I mean is, none of them seemed to know anyone who'd be prepared to come in here, to come and look in on you." He paused for a moment as if trying to work out just how to put what he was going to say next. "Almost like, uh, I mean, kind of like they were all too busy."

"Hmm," Henrietta said, "it's my work phone."

She located her phone, saw that it was still switched on, though the battery was running extremely low. Just a percent or two remaining.

A couple of missed calls. Unrecognised numbers.

Ad agencies were *always* calling her up.

Bastards.

She saw that she still had her map app open. It showed her current location, which turned out to be Himmersmile General Hospital. She paused a moment, thinking it over, and then she zoomed out a couple of times. Saw the green blob.

That brought it all back.

Brought back *just* where she been heading.

And why.

A FEW HOURS LATER, and after having a fairly thorough examination from a lady doctor, who turned out to have better shoe-sense than the male nurse . . . though, considering how much Henrietta knew about hospital protocol, the poor nurse might not have had any choice . . . she emerged out down on the street.

'Back to street level', the slightly giddy thought struck her.

Of course, her first action was to call back those unrecognised numbers on her phone. To speak with those people who had scheduled an interview with her. Her interview with *Streaker Fashions*. The opportunity of her lifetime.

They had been apologetic, but they claimed that they had already selected another candidate. Just as those missed calls suggested, they had tried to get in touch but to no avail.

And so they'd simply given up.

It was like a nightmare.

No . . . it *was* a nightmare.

This was what she had strived for ever since she had ripped open her first doll on a Christmas morning and duly spent the rest of her adolescence dressing her, and her swiftly acquired cohorts, in designs of her own imagining.

And now it was gone.

Oh, sure, there were other design firms. Other places she could apply. But she knew how tight-knit the fashion community was, how she would now have a reputation as a diva with just about every place about town . . . and, anyway, none of those places was *Streaker Fashions*.

No, all her dreams had been built on *Streaker*.

And now that dream was in tatters.

All because of that . . . that *pissing* car. That honking, beeping prick who'd made her stumble. Caught her off guard. Made her bump her head and end up in hospital.

Once she got back to her apartment, she took a forty-minute shower and then made herself a strong, black coffee in her kitchenette. She breathed it in deep as if it was a breathable scouring pad, to strip away that unpleasant medicinal taste that the hospital had inflicted on her. Then she stood leaning out of the window, steaming cup of coffee in one hand, and resting against the rough, paint-flecked, cobweb-ridden window ledge with the other, staring down onto the sun-streaked street below, to the cars meandering past, engines humming along.

And those *idiot* drivers all smugly going about their days.

They probably didn't even *have* dreams.

Of course she hadn't been so ego-drunk as to presume that she would've even got the job if she'd turned up at the interview, but at least she would've had a chance. A chance to fail. But that *pissing* driver had stripped her of even that.

She had wondered what she might do if she didn't manage to get the job at *Streaker*, and she had resolved, beforehand, that she would simply go off and try something else entirely.

Because, for Henrietta, if she couldn't have *Streaker* then she was better off with nothing.

The fact remained, though, that she had nothing lined up. She had no Plan B. And that scared her more than anything else. All her life, her focus had been turned to, first, becoming an international sensation as a fashion designer and, a little later, second, to her linking up with her soul mate, *Streaker Fashions*.

Now, though, nothing.

Nothing at all.

Totally cut free of all her dreams, all her ambitions.

Just like that.

But that driver. That got her thinking.

Revenge?

Was that on the cards?

Should she . . . could she, perhaps, track him down somehow, make him *suffer* in some way?

It would be something, at least, to focus her mind.

Just something to take her mind off desolation for a little while.

What else did she have to do while she worked out just what to do with her life?

Back at the hospital, the doctor had given her his number, so that she might call if she felt any further symptoms, if the concussion made itself felt again. Now, though, that number would serve for another reason . . . a potentially *evil* reason.

And so she dialled her up. Got her on the line. Had the doctor transfer her to someone in the hospital who could give her the contact details of those who had witnessed her accident, on the basis that she was going to go to the police . . . and, strictly speaking, Henrietta hadn't ruled out going to the police, not yet, though she had to admit to herself that it was somewhat at the back of her mind for the time being.

And, anyway, what exactly could they charge the driver with?

Beeping with undue care?

. . . Oh, what did she know about it all. She didn't even drive herself. And, what was more, she had no intention of *ever* learning. She didn't *need* to know all of those rules.

But, nonetheless, she knew a tosspot driver when she saw one.

When she *heard* one.

She got the contact details. Got them all typed out on her phone. The address all written down, and fed into her GPS, and she was on her way.

On her way to extracting some revenge.

Just a little.

4

FOR SOME REASON, maybe just to heighten the drama, Henrietta waited till night time.

Or maybe it had to do with her wanting to make sure her mind was clear—or clear*er*—so that she knew for sure that she wasn't doing this on the back of some rogue psychopathic element buried deep within her beleaguered brain.

She decked herself out in all black: tracksuit trousers, trainers, turtleneck sweater, and, looking at herself into the full-length mirror, she thought that she resembled Catwoman somewhat.

No mask, though, that might be a problem considering the bizarre, illicit plans she had in mind.

She rummaged about in her drawers and managed to dig up a balaclava.

Woolly. Black. And, now that she thought hard on it, once belonging to a long-forgotten boyfriend . . . Daryl? Darrin? Darwin? . . . She seemed to recall, vaguely, that he'd been Australian, or had the trace of an Australian accent, or maybe he'd just been to visit Australia once . . . or had he left her for an Australian girl, or had *she* left *him* for an Australian guy?

Not worth thinking about.

The important thing was the balaclava.

All ready and dressed, she headed out on the town. Not wearing the balaclava yet, though, of course. She took the metro to the part of the city where she'd got the directions on where the driver lived. The address he'd registered on his witness statement.

When she came up for air, the night breeze blew warm against her cheeks, and she could still taste the tomato-and-cheese pasta sauce she'd got down her before coming out. The air smelled fresh, much fresher than it did around her place, what with all the

Chinese and Indian restaurants, and the chippies, the air back round her place was slimy with grease.

The road itself was lined with fir trees. All of them sprouting up out of holes in the bricked pavement. Each tree had neat, tar-black iron railings surrounding it, and the bushy leaves sprouted out over the top and upwards into the sky so that there were patches of pavement where the dim orange streetlights couldn't get through, and those patches were left in shadow.

The leaves rustled slightly in the night breeze, and Henrietta withdrew her phone from the zip pocket of her black tracksuit bottoms, and she flipped to the map, where she'd programmed just where the driver was to be found according to the directions she'd got from the hospital.

She traced the numbers, looking up from the map only to check her footing, that she wouldn't be about to step her nice, fairly new, black trainers into a pile of dog turd. Though, from the looks of this neighbourhood, what with its neat, terraced houses, with those half dozen concrete steps leading up from the street, the railings about *everything*, she guessed that dog turds were the least of her worries.

Finally she found the house.

Checked it, and then double-checked it with the map on her phone.

This was the place.

She took in the façade of the house, the navy blue front door with its brass doorknob in the centre, its brass letterbox. And then the nicely painted cream walls. She thought of that shade of cream as a little like the inside of a shell, just the tiniest hint of pink in there. The window ledges were painted a navy blue too, apparently to match the door.

At least someone here had a sense of colour coordination.

A single light glowed out in the window above the door, sending a shimmering, yellowy glow down onto the steps which led up to the front door, and to where Henrietta had her left foot perched.

She looked to the rest of the house. No other lights lit, and she reached the conclusion that this was supposed to be a simple trick, a trick to try and tell any would-be burglar that the driver—and family?—were well and truly at home, and *awake* . . . when the truth was that they were most likely all snoring away in their beds.

What to do now?

What was her next move?

Look at her here. She'd come out here all this way. Got herself all dolled up . . . in a way . . . and now she was standing about near to midnight on a stranger's street just fussing about what to do next.

She turned her attention to the side of the house. She saw that there was a gravel driveway which ran alongside, and a little further along, a garage door. Again, the same navy blue as the front door.

Was the car inside the garage?

Perhaps.

But what could she do with the car?

She dipped her hand into her pocket. Brought out her key ring, bustling with keys for various nooks and crannies of her apartment, and she examined them in the dim streetlight.

Really? *Really?* Was she seriously considering breaking into the garage and *keying* the driver's car? How old was she? Twelve, thirteen years old? That wouldn't be any sort of revenge. That wasn't likely to teach the driver a lesson at all.

No, she had to come up with something a little worthier.

Something that would actually have an *impact*.

But what?

What was she going to do right now?

Just as she was about to back away, to retreat to her apartment, to go better think over just what she was going to do, she heard the *snick* of the lock on the front door.

Dazed, she glanced upwards, and felt her stomach dip down hard. The taste of pasta sauce at the back of her throat gave her a burning, acidic sensation now, and every bone in her body was telling her to run.

But she just couldn't.

She was rooted to the spot.

The front door opened, and someone emerged.

She took a moment or so to realise just who it was.

The driver.

Of course it was . . . who else would it be?

She was the one who'd come out to his house here, just what had she expected to happen?

He was dressed in a silky white dressing gown that glimmered a little in the glow from the streetlights, and he had a scowl fixed onto his forehead. "You a burglar, then?" he said, his voice quick and to the point, not scared at all . . . or maybe he was just a good actor.

Henrietta felt her heart flutter in her throat. All of a sudden she could smell her clean sweat, that salty odour, wafting up at her. She couldn't think of anything to say.

"If you are," he said, "then you might be better served shoving off elsewhere, you've been rumbled here. The missus has seen you standing about out here for the past fifteen minutes, looking our place over. Why don't you hop it right now before I call the police, eh?"

He took a step forwards. Over the threshold.

He was wearing a pair of sable slippers, they looked moleskin, though Henrietta couldn't be totally sure in such low light. As she turned her attention upwards she saw that he had greasy, black strands of hair combed over to cover his otherwise bare scalp. And it was right then that his mouth opened wide to reveal rows of yellowed teeth, with the odd black mark of decay thrown in for good measure.

"Hey," he said, "think I've seen your face before, haven't I?"

It was only then that she remembered the balaclava, that it was still stuffed into the pouch of her turtleneck sweatshirt. She could feel its bulge at her stomach.

"Yeah," he said, taking another step closer. "You were that dizzy bitch who took a tumble on that zebra crossing, aintcha?"

For some reason, Henrietta detected that the driver's tone had somewhat shifted. Whereas before he'd tried to speak cleaner, to keep a well-hidden accent out of his voice, it was showing through the cracks now that he was apparently caught up in this.

Henrietta took a step back. Then another.

"Whatcha doin' here, eh? At my house?"

His features darkened, and she watched him dip into the pocket of his dressing gown. Even though the light level was low, she could clearly see what it was.

A kitchen knife.

Her heart throbbed hard. Bounced against the confines of her ribcage.

That cheese-and-tomato pasta sauce that had seemed so rich and thick before was now pumping its way up her gullet, burning as it went, filling her mouth with the taste of bile.

The night breeze had grown impossibly hot and she could feel a sensation like a thousand pinpricks jabbing into her skin all over.

A ringing started up in her eardrums, and she struggled to hear the driver's next words, but she did, and when she heard them, she obeyed.

Double time.

"Hop it," the driver said.

5

F OR SOME REASON, Henrietta spent the next week growing increasingly paranoid. She worried that, perhaps, the driver would call up the hospital, that he might somehow be able to get hold of *her* details, and that he would come by to take some sort of revenge on her . . . for the revenge she had taken herself.

Or *tried* to take.

Considered taking.

She padded about her apartment barefoot, over the plush, shag-pile carpet that she'd saved up for weeks—months?—to afford, just so that she could add a touch of class to the place. As she went back and forth for what seemed like the millionth time that morning, a thought struck her. She stopped dead. Scrunched up her toes, squeezed the curls of the shag pile between them. It was kind of like stroking a dog with her feet. Burying her feet in its lush coat.

The first thing that had struck her was the fact that she had money. That she had some pretty substantial savings still sitting around in the bank. Enough money for her to take a course of some kind. To get herself back on her feet.

And it was while she'd been thinking over that fact, thinking over just what she might want to be, that it had struck her out of the blue.

Why didn't she try to understand?

Why didn't she try to see things from the driver's perspective?

From those drivers who blared their horns every day?

. . . And, really, there was only one way for her to see things from their side of the wheel, workwise, and that was to become a mechanic.

A *car* mechanic.

As she sat herself at the wooden bar stool in her kitchen, curling the white plastic phone cord about her index finger, she pondered about how this just seemed to make sense.

What she needed wasn't *revenge*. It was *empathy*.

And, after all, she *had* been looking for a change in life path, wanting to get herself off to something completely different.

She couldn't think of a starker difference between a fashion designer and a car mechanic.

With the telephone directory all spread out across her lap, weighing her knees down, she listened to the *purr* in her ear. The dial tone.

She breathed in the gentle cinnamon smell of her apartment, from the air freshener she used. It made her tongue tang a little. Made her salivate a little, and she wondered if she'd been eating right the past week . . . she had lost count of the amount of meals she'd skipped just from thinking things over. From staring into mid-air.

But the time for thinking was over.

Now she was taking positive action.

She was sorting herself out.

She spoke with the person on the other end, the course instructor, and she gave him her details, told him everything he needed to know to get her signed up.

He took her payment information.

Though she did detect a slight rise in the tone of his voice, as if he was on the brink of breaking out into a full-out laugh, he kept it in, at least until she had hung up with the course all mapped out.

All ready to start the next Monday.

When the day finally did roll around, she dug out her roughest of rough clothes that she could find, not particularly easy seeing as she'd dedicated herself so full-bloodedly to her fashion life. But she managed to find those same black tracksuit bottoms, those same black trainers that she'd put on to go out to the driver's house. She decided to skip the balaclava, though, guessing that the course instructor would have a hard time already dealing with a *woman* on the course, let alone one wearing a balaclava.

She turned up and found herself in a class mostly consisting of male teenagers between the ages of sixteen and seventeen, all of them with some level of facial hair, ranging from man-boy fluff to all-out Tarzan.

Though there were some titters . . . or whatever the male, adolescent equivalent to titters is . . . she soon found herself blending in relatively easy. It helped that they all got served with the same overalls. With the same *colour* of overalls: a light, slightly institutional, grey, though, as the instructor assured them, it was a better colour when dealing with oil and grease and other unpleasantness around the cars.

6

AFTER A LITTLE WHILE, Henrietta managed to find a job with a local dealer, just down the road from her apartment, within walking distance actually. And she was glad that it negated the need to take the metro *anywhere*.

This car mechanic lark seemed to be turning out to be somewhat a stroke of genius.

And she grafted. Learned day in and day out. Did her best. Learned much faster than the other apprentice the dealer had taken on there, and soon enough she found herself with a world of opportunity at her feet, that she was skipping her way upwards in the world.

Once she'd got herself a good amount of money tucked away, enough to fund a good year's worth of a serious venture, she cut herself loose and started up her own operation.

And that operation spiralled out.

She bought up more places.

More premises.

And got extremely rich.

Said none-too heartfelt of a goodbye to her boxy studio apartment.

The buying continued.

She spread her influence even further.

Bought up more and more dealerships, and garages, and—who would've known it?—pretty soon she was one of the most influential businesswomen . . . no, business*people* . . . in the country.

She had power. For the first time in her life.

And she was only just really learning how to wield it.

Soon enough she found herself getting political. That *was*, politicians coming to her. Wanting hand-outs in exchange for influence.

But what would she want with influence?

She had only got into this whole game because she'd wanted to understand.

Because she'd wanted to *empathise* with car owners. To see things from their perspective. To see just *why* they felt that need to toot on their horns. To make innocent, ambitious ladies tumble over, to *ruin* their careers.

. . . Or was she still single-mindedly focussed on revenge?

Because that might've explained away just why she was working on the top-secret project. Why she hadn't seen a need to tell anyone else within her company about it. And how she'd wanted to keep it totally personal.

Because the reasoning behind the project was personal.

And she was *certain* that it would change the world for the better.

At least for other women like her.

Dressed in a smart, no-nonsense lilac trouser suit, Henrietta gazed down on the city from her penthouse on the sixteenth floor of the building she had only purchased in the last month. She looked down at the city through the tinted windows as it curved away from her. Like looking into a glass ball held over a paper map, she could see the streets bending away from her, the traffic streaming about the roads.

And the occasional *hooonk!* of a car horn.

Of a driver.

She sipped on her cappuccino, which her maid had brought to her fresh only a couple of moments before. The milky froth was just perfect. Melted on her tongue. And the mixture not at all bitter. Just soft, kind of like a velvet-tongued lover kissing her with extreme care. The warmth ran through her blood, and up to her brain, and she knew that now—*finally*—the time for revenge had come to her.

After all these years.

All these *decades*, she had finally come to the point where she would be able to make that difference of hers. Release her secret project upon the unsuspecting world.

There was a *buzz* in the distance of her apartment, and when she went to answer, she found herself face to face with Jerremy Hawksman: Minister for Transportation.

Though Henrietta had spent so much time in the world of cars, she hadn't forgotten her fashion roots. Though she was well into her sixties now.

Today, Jerremy was wearing a charcoal-grey suit with a neat light pink, broadcloth shirt beneath. He wore his matching charcoal-grey tie in a Winsor knot, and gave her a broad smile as he took her in, his rosy cheeks getting even rosier.

And his gut seeming to convulse outwards a fraction more.

He swooped in to give her a kiss on either cheek, and then they headed on down through the building, to the floor which she had reserved for her special, top-secret project.

The project that she would reveal to Jerremy today.

To get to the floor—the seventh—she had to use her thumbprint and a retinal scan. She noticed Jerremy looking on with a wry smile, a slight sparkle in his eye.

She wondered if he'd still be smiling once she'd shown him the project.

They emerged on the seventh floor, onto the thin carpet. She flipped the lights, bringing that harsh fluorescent glow to bear on everything.

There, in the centre of the floor, sat the car.

A normal hatchback, a light turquoise, and the one which she had used to create her prototype. And the one which would be used to model the rest of production on.

It was nothing flashy at all.

Three doors. Fairly boxy, just like her studio apartment had once been. But a good runner, and the bestseller across the range she owned, that she manufactured.

Henrietta breathed in deep, savouring the thick metal-and-oil stench down here. Those scents had come to mean more to her than she could ever have imagined. From the amount of time she'd spent down here, often in the small hours of the morning after all the business had been done for the day.

Those scents had represented the culmination of her dream.

She glanced back at Jerremy, still tasting that frothy milk in her mouth. She could see a few worry lines burrowed into his forehead, and she knew that he must be confused. That he didn't have much of a clue about what was going on here.

But he had no need to fear.

She would explain everything quite clearly.

He took another few steps forwards, and then stopped, about five or six paces from the turquoise hatchback as if it might do him some evil if he got any closer. He slipped her a sidelong glance. "So?" he said. "What's all this about?"

She only smiled back at him. "Get in."

He held back another moment.

Henrietta guessed, like most politicians, it was a rare day that Jerremy had to do his own driving. To be honest, she never much did her own either, more from a safety perspective than anything else.

In an apparent leap of confidence, he reached out, undid the handle to the driver's door, and then took his place behind the wheel. He kept the door open and said to her, while looking in front of him, "There aren't any keys here."

"No?" Henrietta said. "Maybe that's because you won't need them."

"What?"

"The main feature of this model is the horn."

He scrunched up his eyes, gave her a cautious glance, and then rested the heel of his hand on the spot for the horn.

She nodded to him reassuringly.

He paused another moment and then depressed the horn.

A sharp, flat *beeeep!* rattled the blacked-out windowpanes.

And the sound echoed about the floor.

Henrietta crunched her teeth together, still unable to separate the sound of a horn from that fateful day. But she kept enough of her wits about her to turn and look back to Jerremy, still seated behind the wheel, in the driver's seat.

The look on his face was priceless, almost as priceless as the pig-like shriek he gave, and how all the hairs on his head seemed to stand upright.

All the colour faded from his complexion as he turned to look at her, his eyes still wide with shock, a thin film of sweat having broken out on his brow. "What ... what ..."

"Quite simple really," Henrietta said, "just a matter of wiring. The horn, you see, whenever it's blown, sends a sharp, high-voltage electrical shock into the seat of the driver's trousers."

His eyes were round and glassy and confused.

Henrietta just gave him a faint smile back. "It's taken me years to be in a position to bring this into production, not because of the technology, you understand, but more because of the political sway."

Jerremy remained stone-faced, in total shock. Slowly his wits seemed to return to him, and he blinked away his daze. Shaking all over, he helped himself up and out of the driver's seat. Even as he stood at the side of the car, he stared back at it, as if it was going to shock him again ... even though he wasn't sitting in the driver's seat any longer.

Henrietta just smiled. Big and broad and proud ... and just a little smug.

"Oh, this'll revolutionise the country, top to bottom, mark my words. An invention hopefully not too late for its time." She smiled even broader, if at all possible, and added, "What do you think?"

FIRE IN AUTUMN

THIS MORNING I thought Jim was joking. He had a smarmy grin on his face when he told me I'd be covering a male fashion show. I'm a sports reporter. My specialisation is football. Sometimes cricket, occasionally rugby. Never female 'sports', and certainly not fashion shows. But cutbacks mean some creative assigning—round pegs in square holes if you ask me.

For the first time in twenty years of journalism I'm seriously considering chucking in the towel.

Sweat dampens my armpits and my grip tightens on the steering wheel. I gun the accelerator and sweep past a dust-covered lorry transporting loaves of bread. After I've got past them I get right up the arse of this ancient green Mini. Woman driving. Sixty-five miles an hour in the fast lane. A couple of flashes of the headlights and she gets the message. Back over to the slow lane where she belongs. I clench my teeth and give her the finger on the way past.

The motorway opens up ahead of me and I really throttle it. Ninety. A hundred. A hundred and ten. Not bad for an estate. I'm not in a rush or anything but when I get pissed off I drive fast. Only way of loosening the tension in my shoulders.

I eye the sign to Haditch and pull off, stomping the brakes as I approach a roundabout. I look right then jerk the car onward, heading for the Sunset Arena, where this travesty is taking place. Only when I get to the car park do I realise I'm actually going to do this.

As I check out the spaces I take note of the piss-awful parking jobs. A car taking up two spaces. Another parked over three bays. Someone's had the nerve to chain a bike up to one of the posts, blocking off a perfectly good space for a car. Makes me wonder if there's a feminist conference going on—perhaps a support act for the glittery homosexual strutting.

I swing into a space and switch off. I sit there with my hands on the wheel reconsidering what I'm doing, whether I really can resign myself to covering this show.

Deciding to give myself a bit of quiet before the storm, I click on the radio.

Blabber Balls.

Non-stop, twenty-four hour football chat.

I lose myself in the woozy voices. Closest I get to meditation. And then my phone whines its way across the dashboard. 'Paedo Jim' flashes on the handset. My editor. I renamed him this morning.

With a sigh I pick up.

"Al?" Jim says.

"What is it?"

"Are you at the show?"

I wonder if he's wearing a shit-eating grin. Maybe the rest of the office around him, listening in on speaker phone. "I'm in the car park. What you want?"

"I just wanted to say that I know this really isn't your cup of tea and I really appreciate you putting in a shift for us here."

"Uh huh."

"And I promise that I'll put you on the next big match that comes up. You'll be the man."

This brightens my mood a touch. Over the past few weeks this freshly-graduated reporter, a hot little blonde called Diana, has been getting her manicured nails all over the sports pages. Jim, like the paedo he is, thinks it's a great step up for diversity. I have to admit she's a decent writer but, as we all know, that counts for nothing because women know absolute zilch about football.

"Right," I say.

"You know the drill, Al. Just get in there, ask the designers a few questions and give us a neat summary of the show. It's just a regional show, warm-up for next week in London, so they should have time on their hands—don't expect more than a crowd of a hundred."

"Kind of like a reserves' match?"

"Yeah something like that." He pauses. "Might even be interesting, getting your take on things as an outsider. You know, reach out."

'Reaching out', for me, constitutes reporting on a rugby match —watching a bunch of twats beat seven bells out of another bunch of twats. Although I'm unconvinced by Paedo Jim's reasoning, the lure of a big match has given me some light at the end of the tunnel.

I have to stop being a petulant child, bite my lip and just get on with it.

"Speak later," he says and hangs up.

I slip my mobile into my jeans, calm myself listening to a few more minutes of Blabber Balls and then let myself out of the car, shrugging on my lambswool-lined leather jacket.

A honking great banner hangs above the entrance to the Sunset Arena. It's written out in gold, sparkly lettering and reads: Fire in Autumn – The Season's Hottest Male Fashions.

I scoot through reception, flashing my press pass to an uninterested security guard. As I emerge onto a concourse, a gaggle of scantily clad men swagger past. One of them catches me with his elbow and sends me careening into the wall then down to the floor.

I lay crumpled on the polished tiles, rubbing my aching skull, cursing the oaf who knocked me over under my breath.

And then I look up.

A bare-chested man wearing a pair of faded blue jeans peers down at me, smiling. He has the most ridiculous mid-riff I've ever seen. I mean, there are washboards and then there are toast racks. He yanks me to my feet and brushes me down. When he speaks he lisps his words. "I'm stho sorry. It's sthimply a sthcircus today."

He points me along the corridor to the designers' dressing rooms. As I draw closer to the room more men crawl out from crevices and archways, all in some state of undress and all grinning.

I do my best to keep my arms tucked into my sides but I inevitably end up brushing some male skin. Their bodies remind me of a ton of sculptures I saw in an art gallery my wife dragged me to. I rummage for my notepad and scribble down that observation.

If Paedo Jim wants my perspective that's exactly what he'll get.

A scrawled note on the door reads: Wanda Hendrix. Sounds like a sodding porn star. I jot that down too and then rap a couple of times. When there's no response from inside I turn the door-knob and venture in.

A silver-haired woman sits on a reclining, brown leather chair. Two semi-naked men stand at her shoulders while another crouches down at her lap like an obedient spaniel. She's rubbing lotion into his hair.

I cough.

She glances up, unsmiling.

"Mrs Hendrix?"

"Miss Hendrix. Wanda."

I slink closer, not daring to take my eye off the men. I've never trusted unclothed men—don't even dare look at myself naked in the mirror.

I take up a safe position, several feet away from the bare male skin. "I'm from the paper."

"Yes, I gathered that. I was expecting"—she turns her attention away from massaging lotion into the man's head, looks me up and down—"someone different."

"Short-staffed."

"I see."

I take in the clichéd dressing table. The light bulbs dotted around the periphery of the mirror. "So, do you make a living from all this?"

Wanda looks into the mirror, pulls at the loose skin surrounding her eyes and sighs. "Yes." She waves the men away, as if they were dogs begging food from a table. When they've left the room she looks me right in the eye. "Mister . . . ?"

"Thompson. Name's Alan Thompson."

"Mister Thompson. May I ask how many fashion shows you have covered?"

"This is my first."

"Ah."

Silence.

I rack my brains for another question. "Is . . . is there some kind of league for fashion?"

She gives me a blank look.

"You know, like . . . uh . . . football."

"Football?" she says, spitting the word.

"Yeah, is there some way to measure who's the best designer. Like, for example, when you have a show in Milan, does the best designer get points?" I rethink the terminology. "Are they given a *ranking*?"

Her well-painted lips shrink.

I flip to a new page in my notebook and am on the cusp of reeling off another question when another model barges in. He's completely naked. No hair. Shaved all over.

Cock like an under-watered carrot.

Wanda's attention floats onto him. "Yes?"

"There's a problem with the second run. The waistcoat's torn around the back."

"Has Cheryl had a look?"

"Yes, but she says she doesn't want to ruin the aesthetic. She wants you to fix it up."

Wanda rises and follows the model out, without another word to me.

I sit in a chair, waiting.

Ten, fifteen minutes pass by before I realise she's not coming back, so I decide to scout out the terrain.

After a bit of mindless wandering, attempting to stop models or designer-looking people, I give in and make for the arena itself where rehearsals are taking place. I take up a seat in one of the back rows and watch the stage. The catwalk is like a pier leading to a dried up ocean. A group of men prance back and forth, motioning to a man dressed in a white jumpsuit with jet-black hair, who nods at their suggestions.

The jumpsuit man claps his hands together and calls what I presume to be a coffee break.

The models scarper off into the wings.

Just as I rise from my seat the man calls to me.

He leaps off the stage and trots up the stairs. Only when he stands beside me do I realise he must be over six-foot tall. He smells of strawberries and peaches, with a hint of cigarettes. His teeth are so white they're almost blue. "I am Fernando," he says.

"Designer?" I say, doing my best to sound enthusiastic.

"Yes."

I introduce myself and explain the situation, that we're short-staffed—that I'm really a sports reporter.

He nods and pouts in all the right places, then says, "Yes, it sounds quite unfortunate. But maybe it is interesting, yes? A different perspective."

"Maybe."

He twirls his hand in the air. "And what do you make of all this?"

"It's very . . . nice."

"Please tell the truth. People outside fashion say it is so silly. Do they not say it is so silly?"

"I suppose so."

"Do you think it so silly, Alan?"

"Well, yeah."

He stares me right between the eyes, clearly wanting a more elaborate answer.

"To be honest," I say, "I've always felt fashion is for homosexuals and highly-strung women."

His smile widens and he chortles. "Are you married, Alan?"

"Yes."

"And I suppose you don't believe your wife to be one of these 'highly-strung women'?"

"Her idea of 'fancy' is a cup of tea with a spoonful of sugar."

He chuckles. "You say that fashion doesn't influence her life?"

"Nah."

"Does she enjoy shopping?"

"You're a bloody mind reader."

He laughs and slaps his ripped thigh. "Yes, yes! I love the sarcasm. Nobody here has no sense of humour. What a very, such nice change."

I just smile along, hoping he'll get round to giving me a decent quote or two. I'm toying with the idea of running out after this interview. Making up the pissing show. It's not like it's news anyway. Besides, Mike Blee will be on Blabber Balls in half an hour to round up the day's top sports stories. But, at the same time, there's something hypnotic about Fernando—I can't *not* look at him when he speaks.

Fernando jabs his crooked finger at my nose. "When your wife goes shopping she buys clothes. The designers who create those clothes come to these shows. This is where they get from their ideas." Without warning he reaches out and runs his thumb and forefinger up the lapel of my jacket. "But you are perhaps not interested in the new clothes?"

"Nope. Haven't been shopping for five years now."

"Incredible."

"Is it?"

He leans back, craning his neck to take in my profile. "Yes, yes. I can see how I could find something in your figure. I think I have just the thing." He heads down the stairs, beckoning me.

I linger on the spot. "Uh, where are we going?"

"Backstage. Trust me."

My lambswool-lined leather jacket and jeans hang off the back of a chair. All around me everyone is naked. It has the neutral smell of baby oil and concealer. The show is starting in fifteen minutes and I should be out there, with the audience, not here with the models.

Fernando's assistant, Paolo, buzzes around me at a million miles an hour. He pinches fabric, sticks pins in—miraculously avoiding any of my essential appendages—and chatters away non-stop about how 'fabulous' I look.

The mirror doesn't lie, or so the saying goes.

I'm wearing a silk robe which flutters down over my knees, leaving my hairy legs bare. It features multi-coloured splodges and makes me look a little like a festive traffic cone.

Paolo lifts my arm and snaps the measuring tape against my sleeve. Next he approaches my leg. From his kneeling position, he glances up. "Which way do you dress, Mr Thompson?"

"What?"

"Which side?"

Puzzled, I say, "Left."

Paolo slides his hand up my inner leg and brushes my cock. Both of us realise what's just happened but neither of us say anything, which works fine for me.

Beat-heavy music throbs through the backstage walls. It reminds me of the music my teenage daughter plays before going out on the town. And that's when it strikes me that I absolutely cannot do this. If any of the guys on the sports desk get wind of this, see the pictures, my life is over.

Paolo smiles at me and then prods me toward the curtain, and the catwalk.

Male models swoosh past me, returning from their own walks, foreheads sparkling with sweat. Their smiles remain pinned to their faces. And, before I know it, Paolo shoves me out onto the catwalk and I'm striding along, lost in the flashes and grinding music.

Just as Paedo Jim said, the arena's almost empty. Sprinklings of people dotted around the seats, a bit like a youth football match, let alone reserves.

When I reach the end I stop, like a deer in headlights, and then scuffle back for the backstage area. I can already hear the crowd's murmurs rising above the sound of the music and I know I've just made a fool of myself.

I slip back in through the curtain where Paolo gives me a thumbs up and a grin. He helps me back to my dressing area and I take off my robe, put back on my normal clothes. On my way out of backstage, Fernando collars me. "*Alan*! You were simply superb! I have a proposal for you, yes? May I have your email?"

Half-numbed by my catwalk and half-numbed by Fernando's charm, I dish it out to him.

He winks at me, then gives me a pat on the shoulder.

I get into the newsroom around midday the next day to find it all abuzz.

Paedo Jim strides up to me with his plastic smile. No doubt the same one he uses to lure unchaperoned boys down to his basement on Halloween. He claps me on the back and giggles. "Wonderful work, Al, really wonderful."

I slip from his grasp and shuffle over to my desk, where I collapse into my chair.

Paedo Jim half sits and half leans up against the desk, affording me a clear view of his lumpy crotch. "Incredible figures. Really. They speak for themselves. Exactly what readers want in the twenty-first century. Different perspectives. You should see the dialogues breaking out in the comment section."

"Yuh," I say, opening up my email.

"Look, Al, I know I said that I'd give you the big game, but this breakthrough is bigger than all of us. You've really taken us to the next level."

I scan my inbox. Forty-three unread. Approximately half of them have 'LOL', or some combination, in their subject. "I dunno, I just wanna do sport, really."

"Oh no. Not after this. You're our star. It would be foolish to waste. Diana's got the sports page covered. I'd like to get you into fashion full time." He chuckled. "It'd be a riot."

"Yeah, it would, wouldn't it?"

Paedo Jim pats my head twice and then swivels off to go bother someone else.

I take a deep breath and then check over the front page of the website. My picture's there. I stand in my silk robe, panic streaking my face.

I look like a frightened clown.

Next I open up my email account to type out my resignation, and that's when I notice a message from Fernando Sanchez at the top of the pile:

Dear Alan,

You are my inspiration.

I wish to create a whole new line based for the Middle-Aged Man, and I would like that you are to be my centre-piece.

We talk soon,

Fernando

I feel hot breath on the back of my neck. I turn in my seat.

Paedo Jim all over me like a rash, grinning away. "Wonderful news!" he says. "Real Gonzo journalism, hands dirty and all that."

"How should I reply?" I say, deadpan, already knowing the answer.

Paedo Jim stalks off, heading toward the sports section, no doubt to speak with Diana, his star. "Take him up, of course."

I crack my knuckles then count off the months before I can take my pension. Not much chance of that, though, not with a daughter to put through uni.

So I fire off an email to Fernando and the rest is history.

JUMPED-UP KIDS MOST LIKELY ON DRUGS

1

SOMETHING ABOUT THE SCREECHING and the screaming out in the street seemed to suggest, at least to Bianca's mind: THE END OF THE WORLD . . . in big block capitals, just like that.

Though it had just gone three o'clock in the morning, Bianca hadn't been trying to get to sleep. In fact, she'd been studying hard for her test coming up bright and early at nine o'clock tomorrow morning. The subject of the test itself was so dull that it was a challenge for her to so much as *imagine* its contents without feeling her eyelids droop.

So she didn't think about it at all.

She reached out for the flat, flavourless can of energy drink which sat up on her desk. When she lifted it, she found it strangely light, and realised that it was empty. She looked about her for some other form of sustenance, but found nothing but chocolate bar wrappers and screwed-up underwear spread all about the floor.

When she breathed in, she caught a strong scent of perfume that she'd sprayed about the place in the hope that it might get the stench of damp out of her bedroom.

One thing was for certain, her landlord didn't quite believe in maintaining the properties he owned . . . to say the least.

She gave a yawn, long and hard, and involuntary, and then she helped herself up to her feet. She drew her dressing gown tighter about herself—about the pyjamas she wore beneath—and she trod lightly over to her bedroom window.

With a light touch, she drew back the curtain just a little and peered out.

Down into the street.

As she looked down there, she saw her fellow curtain-twitchers all catching a peek too.

Retired men.

Mothers.

Children woken by the ruckus.

They all stared out into the street, trying to see what was going on, what had brought them around from their slumber.

Bianca followed all their gazes, and took in the group of kids at the other end of the street.

The orange flicker of the streetlights set their faces in a sort of distorted shadow, and Bianca could see that—unbeknownst to her at the time—it had been raining. The pavements were all slick with rainwater. Making an almost pretty crystalline sparkle in the streetlight.

Bianca tried to get a better look at the kids, but they moved too quickly.

When she tried to count them, she seemed to reach only four or five before they would fan out, or scatter. And she would have to start again.

Some of her neighbours were calling out to the kids, of course they were, but Bianca held back. She'd always made it a crusade of hers never to scold children. It just didn't seem her place. For her, kids should just be allowed to run the surface of the Earth, their behaviour unchecked, their actions unquestioned. When they hit eighteen years old, of course, it became a different matter. Because then they would be *adults* . . . but till they reached that point, Bianca was of the mind that society should cut kids some serious slack.

Stop trying to make them into the contented, idiot workers that seemed to occupy the entire planet.

Contented, idiot workers just like her.

. . . *Oh, to be a child again!*

It was with that thought on her mind, and those images of the kids skittering back and forth, apparently without any sort of order or organisation, that Bianca took one glance at the opened textbook lying flat on her desk . . . the textbook that, even with months of studying, she had only managed to get about halfway through . . . and she made her choice.

She padded down the stairs, taking care not to wake her sleeping housemates.

They really *were* sound sleepers.

She wondered if they used earplugs and those eye shades they handed out on planes.

Perhaps.

Bianca hooked her long coat off its hook and draped it about her shoulders. With a final, decisive tug of her dressing gown cord —making sure that it was nice and tight about her waist—she shipped on out through the front door, taking care to slip the key out and put it in her pocket as she went. It wouldn't do for her to get caught on her doorstep at three in the morning without a key . . . having to ring the doorbell and get her housemates up to let her in.

That wouldn't do *at all*.

2

THE EARLY MORNING was pleasantly chilly, and Bianca could feel its cold kiss up against her cheek. It didn't send a shudder right down to her blood as she had expected it to. She still had that flavourless taste of the energy drink in her mouth, though she noted gladly that she seemed to be swiftly leaving it behind as she breathed in the clean air.

She listened for the shrieks and giggles. She could feel the eyes of her fellow curtain-twitchers on her, and she wondered if they shared her fantasy of stepping out of their voyeuristic shoes and into the ones of the actor.

If they wished to join her then she could have no complaint.

But none of them did.

She guessed that the best most of them had by way of becoming actors out here was to have the phone to their ear and the finger hovering over the autodial for the police.

Bianca strode along the pavement slick with sweaty rain. She felt good in the bulky walking boots she'd decided on. They were caked with mud, a little of which flaked off with each of her footsteps. She could hear the kids again now, instinctively knew that they were just up ahead, hiding out in the park.

As she stepped through the metal bars which made up the rudimentary fence surrounding the park, she wondered if she was maybe making a mistake.

If she was somehow putting herself into danger.

When she glanced back over her shoulder, back along the street, she saw that the curtain-twitchers had gone, for now, that the volume had once more crept back down to an acceptable level . . . that the ruckus had reached an end for the time being.

But she was certain that if the kids were to return, the curtain-twitchers would be back just as quickly. And the whole stalemate would play out again on the street.

Bianca felt her boots squelch a little as she stepped onto the grass, and she guessed it had been raining just a little harder than she had thought. She glanced about herself, into the darkness of the park—only the odd streetlight here or there to light her way—and she tried to catch sight of the kids.

They alerted her to their presence with the flicker of lighters.

Tiny flames as they lit their cigarettes . . . or *were* they cigarettes?

Once again, Bianca reminded herself just what she was doing. Where she was right now. That she'd left the peace and quiet of her early-morning studies, for an exam she had first thing in the morning, to come along and cavort with a whole bunch of jumped-up kids most likely on drugs.

. . . So?

The kids were over by the swing set. She could hear their chuckling even from where she stood. She wondered if it was meant to be intimidating. If she was meant to feel *threatened* by the kids all over there. Now that she did a rough count, she was sure there must've been eight or nine. All of them boys from what she could tell.

But Bianca kept on striding forwards—coming closer and closer to them.

As she closed the gap, she felt the first sense of apprehension, her heart missing a beat. But she pressed onwards. Drew her arms over her chest for warmth.

The smell of smoke . . . and she could smell now that it was *marijuana* smoke . . . was overwhelming as she stepped closer to them. It was only when she took the final steps, when the sole of her boot trod over the softened mat of the kids' playground that she felt her old confidence return to her. That feeling she'd had back sitting up in her bedroom.

Looking down into the street.

"Hi," she said, breaking the silent stare of the kids.

None of them said anything.

One of the kids uttered a swearword under his breath.

It didn't intimidate Bianca.

In fact, she was feeling so confident of her dominion over them that she had the presence of mind to take in their appearances. Their tracksuits, their baseball caps drawn down over their brows, and the way that, if they weren't holding a joint, they'd stuff their hands into their pockets.

"Whatcha want?" one of the braver kids asked.

Bianca looked to the kid who had spoken and she smiled at him.

He didn't smile back.

For some reason, she found herself put in mind of Snow White and the Seven Dwarfs. Was this the fantasy that she hoped to play out here?

Perhaps her colleagues were right when they'd often tell her to her face that she was a bit of a ditz, a *daydreamer*.

But the truth of the thing was that she was *different* to them.

She couldn't simply put her mind on hold while she went through a whole mindless day of work. She couldn't do that at all. She needed to allow herself some room to breathe.

Else she might suffocate.

Bianca did her best to act nonchalant as she said, "I just came down here to see what was going on."

The same kid snorted back some phlegm and then spat at his feet.

It wasn't a threatening act—more like he was just taking care of a bodily necessity.

That was the thing with marijuana, Bianca recalled from her student days, that it had a nasty habit of making your spit cram up into thick, sticky wads.

"Yeah?" the kid said, coming up from air following his deposit. "And whatcha gonna do now, go off crying to the police, or wha'?"

Bianca studied the kid's face. She tried to work out just who he thought she was. Of course, what with her getup, and the way that she had trekked out here obviously dressed for bed beneath her coat, that all seemed to suggest that she was the stereotypical *intense* neighbour. And yet, at the same time, she knew that she wasn't.

"No," Bianca said. "I'm not going to call the police."

"Then whadja want?"

This time the kid had a bit of a strain on his voice, like he was beginning to lose his temper. Another of the kids, though, tried to calm him down.

"Aintcha ever heard of bein' polite, Jeff, huh?"

The kid who'd spoken first—Jeff, apparently—now took on a somewhat sheepish expression.

Bianca felt a little sorry for him in a way, that one of his own friends had snapped at him. She realised that these sorts of kids acted sort of like a pack of wolves, and that status in the group was just about everything to them.

"Wha's your name?" the kid who'd scolded Jeff said.

"Bianca," Bianca said.

There was a round of giggles from all the kid. Somebody passed the spliff along. Another puff of smoke rose into the early-morning air.

"What?" Bianca said, not feeling affronted particularly, but keen to try and understand the joke. "What's funny about my name?"

"Yuh know," Jeff said, doubled over and still laughing a little while others about him were totally losing it, "Just sounds funny, dunnit?"

Bianca pouted. "I never really thought about it."

It was only when she spoke up that Bianca realised there was a girl among them. She was dressed like the boys and overweight.

Bianca supposed that the tracksuit really didn't do her figure any favours.

"Is you posh?" the girl said.

Bianca wasn't sure what to say to that.

"Just that Bee-ank-uh sounds like a posh name."

Again, Bianca wasn't really sure if this was meant as some kind of a threat. She couldn't detect any sort of malice from the girl's voice, but who knew what sort of contempt they held for 'posh' people?

"What's your name?" Bianca said to the girl, trying out a counterstroke.

"Fernanda," she said.

In the darkness, lit up only by the odd flare from the end of the spliff, Bianca tried to make out some aspect of Fernanda's facial structure that might suggest some Latin heritage. But, no, there was nothing. Nothing that Bianca could see, anyway.

One of the kids—one of the *boys*—hocked long and hard, and then spat on the mat below his feet, the mat that was supposed to stop kids from breaking bones if they slipped off the swings or overindulged themselves on the way down the slide.

Bianca met Fernanda's eye, and Fernanda rolled her eyes at her. Bianca supposed that Fernanda was probably fed up of hanging around with just boys . . . because Fernanda didn't seem, to Bianca, to be one of those proverbial 'girly-girls'.

Bianca started to feel a little more accepted into the group. She could feel the gentle chill of the night-time air up against her cheeks. Right when she was on the point of asking for a toke, one of the kids shoved the spliff in her direction.

"Want some?" he said.

Bianca looked to Fernanda, who was giving Bianca another roll of the eyes, and then Bianca accepted the spliff anyway. As Bianca brought the spiff up to her lips, sucked in deeply on the strange-tasting smoke, she couldn't help but wonder when was the last time she'd consumed any sort of a drug . . . besides alcohol, of course . . . had it been back at university? Or had she been a naughty girl a shorter time ago?

Oh well, it didn't really seem to matter as she took the heavy smoke down into the very base of her lungs, and felt it prickle against the inside of her chest. Already, as she passed the spliff onto another of the kids waiting on the swings, she could feel herself getting light-headed. And it was then that she thought it the right time to confide in her new . . . well, she supposed that she could think of them as *friends*.

"I've got an exam early tomorrow morning," Bianca said, and then really felt like throwing herself backwards, spreading her arms across the dew-tipped grass.

3

NONE OF THE KIDS seemed to have an answer to Bianca's statement . . . it *had* been a *statement*, after all . . . there had been no sort of an intonation, nothing to suggest that it *should* provoke a reply, and well . . . God. Was she stoned? Was that what she felt like now? Her feet light, her heart reduced to a gentle *thump-thump* in her eardrums, and her mind seeming to be just about a million miles away from here. Unrestricted by space and time.

One of the boys tossed the expired spliff down on the ground, then, as he got up off his swing, he stretched his arms up to the night sky. He looked about his friends and they all got up onto their feet too.

Some little part of Bianca spoke to her—told her that she should watch out.

That she should be on her guard.

But she dismissed that voice just as soon as she'd heard it speak to her.

And she turned her attention to the kid who'd got up onto his feet.

He was looking back off towards the street—towards Bianca's street, the street which she called home. He gave a hard sniff that seemed to drag quite a significant amount of mucus along with it. "Shouldn't you get to bed?" he said. "I mean, if you've, like, gotta exam tomorrow?"

To begin with, Bianca felt a little tickled about his concern, the way that he said 'exam' as if it was a word borrowed from a foreign language. She found herself smirking just a touch. She shook her head. "Nah," she said, "I'm thinking of quitting my job, actually."

The boy stayed still. His baseball cap kept his face in shadow, maintained his eye sockets like deep, dark, unfathomable pits.

When he spoke again, his voice was so quiet that Bianca guessed he didn't want the others—his *friends*—to hear.

"Had exams once."

"Yeah?" Bianca said, too loudly, and she saw that the kids watching on, gathered around, would've surely heard her.

"Mm, back at school"—the kid sniffed . . . but not in a way that suggested he was trying to cover tears, more like a way that he was still feeling the effects of the joint he'd been sucking on—"had some exams to finish, you know what I did?"

Bianca shook her head.

The kid shrugged. "Didn't go."

"Why not?" Bianca said.

"Didn't feel like it."

Bianca felt a touch uncomfortable—almost like her skin had got itchy all of a sudden—as the other kids all stood up and surrounded the two of them. Her mind giddily spun back to a time when she'd been studying for her history degree, back at school, and how she'd done a whole module in anthropology—looking into what might well have been Neanderthal societies.

For some reason she felt almost like she'd travelled back in time, like she'd simply shot all the way back to the Stone Age—or whenever Neanderthals had lived, she hadn't got a very good mark on *that* module. It was like something out of a film. Like she was this girl who'd travelled back in time to meet with these . . . *more basic*—that sounded right, didn't it?—beings.

Bianca realised that, from beneath his baseball cap, the kid was still staring hard at her, that he was hitting her with something of a *searing* gaze. "Uh," she said, quickly trying to bring her mind back on track, "And you never thought of *retaking* the exams?"

"Nah," the kid said. "Do all right—not got much, but I do all right."

Bianca speculated as to what that really might mean. If the kid meant that, on his Jobseekers' Allowance, he got by nicely. That he could get himself watered and fed and then have a little change left over to spend on . . . what had they called them back in the day . . . *eighths?*

Suddenly, she felt an almost motherly urge at the base of her gut. Something which seemed to seize hold of her, and not let go. And, before she could really control herself, she said, "Would you like somebody to help you take those exams again?"

The boy was quiet for a long time, and Bianca was certain that his friends, gathered around him, had heard exactly what she'd said. At the same time she wondered why they weren't starting into him, why they weren't 'having a go' at him . . . bringing him down a peg or two. It was only then that she realised that they were viewing this situation here—this experience of Bianca being out of bed at what must've been past four o'clock in the morning— as something approximating a religious experience.

Why, if she had had a pin, and she decided to let it slip through her fingers, she was fairly certain it would've echoed all about the park.

Finally the boy answered her question.

"Nah," he said. "Had my chance, din I?"

Bianca didn't know what to say to that. She had never been one much for philosophical debate. She preferred things that she could see and touch . . . which, in retrospect, was probably why she'd elected not to take her history studies any further than pre-grad-uate . . . though she supposed that her less-than-amazing grades had probably also been a factor.

She looked about her, felt her chest rising and falling. It felt like she'd been wrapped in cotton wool now, and a strange sleepiness had descended over her. She looked out over the kids, all of them in that group standing before her. She couldn't quite believe that, only about an hour ago, they'd been running wild through her street, bringing all the curtain-twitchers out of the woodwork.

Time for bed.

And so, with a farewell to her new-found friends, she trudged back off across the park, over the thick grass and the still-sticky mud, and back home.

When she re-entered her house, everything was totally silent. Her housemates snored on into the night—stuck in their dreams. Nothing spectacular had happened for them between the hours of three and four in the morning . . . nothing more spectacular than, maybe, venturing to the toilet.

For Bianca, though, she was certain that something very profound had occurred in those witching hours, out in that park. And though it had been somewhat obtuse, she knew that she would recall standing there, among those kids, for a very long time indeed.

4

THE NEXT DAY, after Bianca had gone through the general morning routine—but still feeling like she was wrapped in cotton wool—she arrived to the office to sit her exam.

Though she did her best as she was going along, scribbling away on the lined paper they'd handed her to write her answer, she couldn't help her mind slipping onto something else. Perhaps it had been the marijuana, or maybe it was something else . . . something else which had been pursuing her for a long time and was only now *finally* catching up.

She didn't do anything mental. She didn't stand up, rip the paper into a thousand little pieces and have herself an impromptu, manufactured blizzard. She didn't bite her pencil in half and then throw it at the old crone half-slumped over her desk at the other end of the otherwise vacated room. No, she simply sat there, and she completed her answer. And when she was done—when the clock had ticked out her time limit—she stood up, with perfect professional grace, and she handed the paper over to said crone and ventured on out, back to her desk, back to her working day.

But even then, sitting at her computer screen, she knew that she had made her decision, knew that, last night, some deeper part of herself had been touched by something . . . no, that wasn't the right way to put it . . . more like *awakened*. That was right, it was more the case that some aspect of her personality—of *herself*—that she had long ago neglected had now been reinspired.

And she would go through the change.

How she'd come out the other end, she really had no way of knowing—who *would* know?—but she got the impression that she *would* change.

And it was with that thought that she skittered out of the office at her usual time—about fifteen minutes before quitting time—and padded off to the bus stop.

As she stood there, waiting for her bus, she couldn't help but notice, across the road, over a fence which encapsulated a park, that she saw a whole bunch of jumped-up kids most likely on drugs all gathered around the children's swing set. And though none of them caught her eye, she knew, at some gut level, just who they were.

And, perhaps more importantly, she knew just who she was too.

LIBRARY OF LOVE

1

SOPHIA could still taste the remnants of her tuna sandwich. It had been one of those wonderful ones—a *real treat*. The one which came with red pepper, and lashings of mayonnaise. Just the rich, *full* smell of it was enough to send quivers through her stomach, and buckle her knees.

Sophia turned her mind back to the present—the sandwich was gone, after all.

Still here. In the University Library.

She gripped hold of the transparent plastic bag provided. It made that plasticky crinkling sound that just drove her nuts. *That* sound of plastic bags crinkling which seemed to come perpetually from the flat of the old woman who lived across the hall from her.

That sound had a habit of waking her up at three in the morning.

Because the old woman had obviously decided that since *she* couldn't sleep, then neither would any of her long-suffering neighbours.

Sophia wondered if she qualified for the *long* part . . . after all, she'd only been living in that dump of place for a couple of months now.

But she certainly *was* suffering.

Next term, she'd find somewhere new, when she had some time to think.

The plastic bag had an impression of the University Library stamped on it in a monochrome black. The shape of the library always reminded her of the Taj Mahal, for some reason. Maybe it was the way it seemed to grow weight as it rose upwards, becoming all bulgy as it made inroads on the skyline.

She placed her mobile phone in the transparent plastic bag.

Next her notepad and pen went inside also. According to the rules of the library, she wasn't allowed to bring in anything other than her writing materials. And the bare essentials. Fortunately, her mobile phone, set to Silent—not even Vibrate—qualified.

The first couple of visits to the library had thrown her—like when she'd turned up with her backpack, and been swiftly informed that she couldn't come inside with it, lest she try to steal some valuable manuscript or—from what Sophia had observed of her visits thus far—think of scooping up a good helping of the sacred dust which lined the place and taking off with it.

She glanced back over her shoulder to the rotating doors of the University Library.

Yes, there he was again.

That handsome, dark-haired chap.

The one who she was *sure* had been following her all the way here.

But she was probably just being paranoid.

After all, she was bookish, with flimsy, pale-blond hair. She had the figure of a well-gnawed, pencil, and not a well-loved one at that.

Her skin burned on days like today—that was when the sun dared to peek on out from behind a fluffy cloud. And it didn't seem to matter how much sun cream she slopped onto herself— those rays always found their way through to her skin.

Always left her with a complexion like a slightly overdone sausage.

And that was before she even got started on her glasses, and how the thick lenses seemed to magnify her pupils by factors of ten.

She looked back to the desk, to the librarian staffing the desk.

A girl who Sophia recognised as being in her year at university. She had seen her about, but their paths had never seemed to cross, though something about her made her think that she was studying something *sciency* . . . physics, chemistry, something like that?

Certainly not *biology*.

Though the girl's clothes changed every time Sophia saw her, there seemed to be a general theme to them, which was to say that the girl always wore the same cotton, V-necked sweater, with the collar of her blouse poking up through the gap.

Today she wore a faint green blouse beneath, and a black sweater on top.

Though the girl was fairly large-framed, she always seemed to wear a sweater about a size too big, as if she thought that might help hide her figure.

But, really, it only drew more attention to it.

Hiding one's figure was something which Sophia knew all about.

Sophia flashed another glance over her shoulder, back to the dark-haired man striding in through the door. She couldn't help but pause for several seconds, even as the girl in the ill-fitting sweatshirt held out her library card to take.

The guy, he was . . . well, fairly dashing.

And yet she was sure, in equal measure, that she was only flattering herself.

That there was *no chance* he had been pursuing her.

That'd teach her to pollute her brain with those romance novels—it'd become a habit that she'd get back to her room and digest two or three in an afternoon.

"Excuse me?" the librarian said, this time *thrusting* the card towards Sophia.

Sophia took it from her, gave her a sheepish grin, and then padded on through the wooden turnstile, and into the library-proper.

When she reached the other side, she couldn't *help* just one more glance back over her shoulder. Just to be sure. And that was when she caught his gorgeous, *silver* eyes.

Blushing all over, she trotted on up the steps and into the book stacks.

In search of anonymity all over again.

2

SOPHIA DUG into the pocket of her jeans, felt her fingertips brush up against the jagged packet of gum she kept there.

It was funny. Being here, in the library, she felt almost like she was back in school.

Of course chewing gum here was *most strictly* off limits, but since there wasn't exactly an abundance of security cameras—let alone *guards*—she knew that she would most likely get away with it.

Still, it did send a thrill through her.

Sort of like those thrills she would get back at school when she was trespassing on some part of the school at some forbidden hour.

Her heart rushing with the prospect that a teacher might round the corner of the corridor at any second and *tell her off*.

She dug out the stick of gum—her last—and she poked it in between her lips, chewing it up and savouring the minty waves which melted into her mouth.

When she breathed out now, she smelled the mint too.

Felt the almost *stinging* freshness as it passed through her nostrils.

Her dampened footsteps on the thick—*ancient*—crimson carpets were the only sound around here, save for when she would step past a stack of books and find some other student—or *reader* —there, poring over some volume.

And then it was only that slick—*crisp*—turn of pages.

As Sophia got towards the end of the corridor, she eyed her destination.

The label which read 'Russian Literature'.

Like some dizzy dormouse, ensuring that there was no

prowling cat about, she glanced back over her shoulder to see if that dark-haired, handsome fellow was still following.

Nope.

No sign of him.

Just like she'd told herself, it'd *all* been in her head.

She sidled on into the stack and immediately found herself back at home.

Yes, this was what it was.

As she passed by the shelves, she read off her old friends from the spines: Chekhov, Dostoyevsky, Pushkin, Lermontov, and, of course, *Tolstoy*.

She camped herself over at the table by the window which looked on out over the overcast, yet brightly lit, car park.

It was another of those late-summer afternoons.

Those afternoons where some of her best friends would be all out there, lying in the long grass, drinking warm cider and laughing helplessly.

But Sophia didn't much like those occasions.

That habit of drinking in the afternoon.

It had a habit of making her feel lazy-minded—*sleepy*, even— and she much preferred the evening forays, them all going out to one of the many cosy pubs throughout town, tucked off in a corner with their glasses of red wine, and perhaps a packet of roasted peanuts.

She breathed in the dusty air here, that unmistakable, *leathery* odour of the books which surrounded her. She had promised herself long ago that, when she finally got her hands on her doctorate, and—if by some minor miracle—managed to land herself a job teaching, or—better—*researching*, she would find herself some quaint little cottage, and take herself out a cute little mortgage.

The first thing she would do would be to allocate one of the rooms as her study, and simply stock it full to bursting with volumes she picked up at second-hand bookshops.

In her mind's eye, she also saw this theoretical study of hers as having constant beams of summer sunshine pouring in through the window.

Bringing out that same smell which she breathed in right now.

She gave her gum another couple of subtle chews, never quite able to let go of the belief that—*just maybe*—somebody might be watching her without her knowing it.

In fact, as she turned to look at the doorway back into the corridor, she saw that, on this specific occasion, there *was* somebody watching her.

The dark-haired, handsome man who she'd believed to be following her.

He was here.

Now.

And standing *there*, and *looking* at her.

"Hello," he said, a slight smile clinging to his lips.

All at once, Sophia felt like her knees had turned to jelly, like her spine was about as significant and secure as warmed-up rubber.

In the panic, she accidently swallowed her gum, feeling that kind of scratchy sensation as it made its way down her throat, leaving her with a flavour somewhere between mint and *bile*.

"Uh, hi," she finally got out.

The way the dark-haired, handsome man was standing—leaning into the doorframe, with one of his arms flailing above his head—reminded Sophia of those male models she'd seen posing in magazines. But she was fairly sure this man wasn't a model. Though *she* found him handsome, she knew—from all the ribbing her girlfriends would give her—that she had quite a *particular* taste in men.

"You very beautiful," the man said, and only now did Sophia

realise how his accent cut into his English—a kind of *brutal* tone of voice.

And no verb *to be* anywhere to be seen.

It felt like Sophia's cheeks were throbbing, and she realised that she must be blushing. She looked away from those silver eyes of his, and to the spines of the books all stuffed into the shelves, as if by merely looking over there—turning her mind back to her work —she might be able to banish this, what was surely some illusion, from her mind.

But it only seemed to encourage him to speak more.

"You must forgive," he said. "I very curious—in the town, I see you, and I think you very beautiful."

There it was again, him using the adjective 'beautiful' to describe her, though she couldn't for the life of her see how *that* might apply at all.

She breathed in deep, thought back to all those things her mother had taught her throughout her girlhood—all those little facts about men, all those things that nobody seemed to speak about, that even her girlfriends never even seemed to speak about . . . the way that her mother had rammed home that she needed to wary of men *at all times* . . . and that they were a Very Great Threat.

But, when she looked into *this* man's silvery eyes, she couldn't help but find herself bound up inside of them—thoroughly ensnared.

Was this what her mother had meant?

"Uh," Sophia said, not really knowing what to do with her hands, so turning to wring her fingers—to open them wide and then crunch them shut again into fists. "*Thank* you," she finally got out.

The man stayed where he was, leaning up against the door-frame, but his gaze now wandered. Over to the book stack. And to the spines of the books.

But he seemed to become bored quite quickly, and his eyes

soon wandered back onto Sophia, and she watched on—helpless—
as his full-blooded, pert lips formed another of those wide smiles.
"What you do here—alone?" he said.

Sophia felt the blood rising into her cheeks all the more. She
took this as her opportunity to break off her gaze with him, to
look back to her notepad and pen, still snug inside the transparent,
monographed plastic bag. "I'm a, uh, *student*," she said.

" 'Student' ?" the man said.

Not really feeling like she could summon the strength to repeat
herself, Sophia settled on a nod.

"Hmm," the man said, "I student *too*—I here for *exchange*."

Sophia raised her eyebrows at this—for the first time in the
conversation, the subject no longer being her 'beauty', feeling like
she had some sort of a foothold. "Oh?" she said. "And what are you
studying?"

The man drew in a sharp breath through his nose, then he blew
it out just as quickly. His eyes again wandered to the spines of the
books, and then snapped right back onto Sophia's. "This and *that*,"
he said.

The slightly idiomatic expression caught Sophia a little off
guard. She'd sort of eased herself into—if 'eased' was the right
word—his manner of speaking.

His smile returned to his lips. "To speak with honesty, I must
say that education, it *bores* me."

Sophia had no idea what to say to this, herself occupying the
complete opposite of his position, so she just did her best to smile
'sweetly' . . . which sort of constituted the smile of her friend Elena,
who she had studied several times over for her *femininity*.

"Yes," the man continued, now looking past Sophia, and out the
window, to the car park, "I think not to stay long here—not
for *study*."

Sophia blinked a few hundred times then decided to take a
plunge. "Well," she said, "I'm hoping to be an academic." She

paused, wondering if she might be giving away too much, then decided that dark-haired, handsome men didn't come across too often in her dormouse life, and said, "I'm studying for my thesis in Russian Literature."

At this point, the man crossed his arms over his chest, and pouted.

Sophia felt like she'd said something wrong—as if she'd just put her foot in it.

When the man spoke again, his voice was gravelly, almost too gravelly for her to make out his words. "I *Russian*," he said.

"Ah," she said, and then, searching for some way to break the icy layer that'd somehow settled on their conversation, added, "What's your name?"

3

I T TURNED OUT that the man's name was Leo, and that he'd arrived here, to the city, about three weeks before. And that, thus far, he was totally uninterested in anything that said city had to offer. It was only when Sophia noticed a beak-nosed librarian shifting towards them, out of the ever-growing shadows of the corridor, that she thought to check the time.

But the librarian negated the necessity of looking at the screen of her phone.

"Closing up in half an hour," she said, and then she looked down her beak at Leo, stuck out her bottom lip, apparently *appalled*, and then she stalked on off to some other nook, or cranny, of the place, waiting out for that sacred—*magical*—time when there would be nobody but herself in the library.

Sophia looked over the bookshelf, and the spines all sticking out, and then she glanced back to the desk, and to her notepad and pencil, both of them very much still snug within the transparent plastic bag.

Where had the time *gone?*

"You like a drink, yes?" Leo said as she took in her unused stationary.

When Sophia looked back to him, she saw that a new steeliness had appeared in his gaze, like he'd seen something that he *wanted* and that he was *determined* that he wouldn't be stopped.

What else could she really have said except yes?

4

THEY HAD NOTHING to talk about as they crunched their way along the gravel path which ran alongside the library building, but Sophia was happy enough to breathe in the freshness of the summer air, what with its slightly *chilly*—September—tang.

It was then that Leo turned to her and began to shrug his coat from his shoulders. He handed it to her, his index finger like a *very well* sculpted wooden hook. "You put this, yes?"

Sophia was a little taken aback by this gesture.

First of all, she wasn't really all that cold.

Had he noticed so much as a spot of gooseflesh, somewhere her skin had betrayed her, something like that?

But she took his coat all the same—a brown leather jacket which was battered in what she'd always considered a 'rock-star' sort of a way.

When she put it on over her shoulders, she could feel Leo's body heat, and it was only then that she realised that, yes, actually, she had been feeling just a slight chill.

She could smell him too—his rich, cologne-inflected scent mixed in with the leather.

As they walked together, she couldn't help but have a stale sort of a taste in her mouth, and she scolded herself for having swallowed her gum.

It had been silly of her.

But she knew that she'd only gone and done it because Leo had caught her off guard.

Why did she have to always be that . . . that *skittish?*

As they walked, side by side, neither of them saying anything at all, she couldn't help but feel herself glowing outwardly. In fact, she couldn't quite pin down a time when she'd felt better than right now. It had been a wonderful feeling to walk past the librarian seated at the reception, in the main hall of the library—the girl who seemed to be in Sophia's year.

That look she'd given her as she'd seen Leo striding along at her heels, well it could quite easily have cut glass.

They proceeded on down the path till they got to the first alleyways of the city—those ancient, snaking passages with cobblestones, and wooden rafters jutting out from the sides of the buildings. Already she could hear the familiar noises of people beyond.

The car horns.

The chattering of pedestrians.

An occasional note from some group of buskers: the string of a violin, the blaring of a trombone, or the beating of a drum.

"Where we go?" Leo said.

For a couple of seconds, Sophia was struck completely and totally dumb.

Because she'd seen her girlfriends.

Over there.

All three of them.

Moving together like a gaggle of geese.

Why she was frightened, she really had no idea, no way of rationalising. Still, she thought quickly, turned her attention back to Leo. "Uh, there's a pub called the *Dummard's Yarn*—this way," she said, indicating with her hand.

She had chosen *that* particular pub because it happened to be in the opposite direction to which her girlfriends were moving.

Leo nodded at her selection.

They moved off in that direction.

As they began on their way down the narrow alleyway on the other side of the street, she had been so sure that they'd managed to escape, that her girlfriends hadn't seen her.

But then she heard, bright and clear, Elena's voice.
"Oh, *Sophia!*"
Her blood ran cold.

5

EXACTLY TWELVE MINUTES LATER—Sophia had
developed a fidget which entailed her checking the screen of
her mobile phone every couple of seconds—they were all sat down
in the *Dummard's Yarn*, her girlfriends all blabbing away at a mile a
minute, their bags of shopping deposited on the benches beside
them, as if acting as stuffing, choking them up against the wood,
keeping them snug there.

Sophia couldn't believe it.

Why couldn't just *one* nice thing *ever* happen to her?

Just *for once?*

And when she'd been least expecting it—when she'd been in the
library, when she'd met with Leo, this *dashing* man.

Now that she was crammed into the wooden bench alongside
him, looking at him in profile, taking in that sculpted jaw of his,
and that—apparently—jet-black hair, she couldn't help thinking
that he was *more* attractive.

Was that just the nature of competition?

That it made the prize all the more tempting?

Sophia hadn't been unaware either of just how Elena was twiz-
zling a strand of her red hair about her little finger, and how she
was giving Leo that doe-eyed stare of hers.

Though Leo had thus far batted back any attempt at flirtation
with that stone-faced glare of his, Sophia was *certain* that one of
her girlfriends—all of them *infinitely* prettier than her—would
steal him away at the last.

Girls like her didn't *win* men like Leo.

She looked to the other two: to Alexa, and Terri.

Alexa's own black hair seemed to be a nutty brown when
compared with Leo's, though her delicate, porcelain features
remained as fetching as ever.

Terri's *blond* hair seemed more brilliantly shiny, much thicker, than Sophia's.

And Sophia knew, if anybody were to place the two of them together—Terri and *her*—that they would objectively pick Terri every time.

Because Sophia knew well that she had nothing beautiful about her.

That was why she'd gone and hidden herself away in books.

All her life.

It seemed like the only way for her to get through life.

The night soon rolled in outside the *Dummard's Yarn*, and Sophia found herself ebbing in and out of the conversation which, unsurprisingly, revolved around the three of her girlfriends attempting to extract various elements of Leo's life story—one mono-syllabic response at a time.

Sophia watched on as the staff of the pub set about lighting up candles, bringing out that orangey, flickering glow to the interior of the place: lighting up the thick, wooden beams, and the rustic, stone surroundings.

More than anything, Sophia itched to get out of here.

To *get away* from her girlfriends.

But she knew that now, surely, it would be impossible.

Why, if she stood up, declared with a smile—*always* with a smile—that she was leaving, that would leave open the opportunity for her girlfriends to sneak in and make their claim . . . she had seen it before, how they would work together, as a sort of three-pronged pitchfork, and stick themselves into the prey they'd picked off for one of them to enjoy later.

But why bother putting it off any longer?

What would it serve to prolong this farce?

One day Sophia assured herself that she would have a good half dozen cats to keep her company, to ward off the loneliness of her evenings, to ease the pain of waiting out the time before the next day spent in the library.

And so, just like that, steeling her nerve, she rose to her feet.

Stood over her girlfriends.

She watched their expressions.

Those *feigned* looks of disbelief.

The ones which inevitably prefaced the polite begging to stay . . . though Sophia well knew that they only wished for *Leo* to stay behind.

So that they might pick at him like a crowd of vultures.

Peck him to the bone.

Then move onto the next carcass.

"Think I'm going to head off, then," Sophia said, surprised at just how weak and pathetic those words of hers had come out.

Her girlfriends were transitioning from the feigned disbelief to the barely-shrouded looks of pity.

And then, just like clockwork—one by one—they looked in Leo's direction, awaiting his response.

Sophia *wouldn't* though.

It was too painful.

To be reminded just how *plain* she really was.

How she was destined to be lonely for the rest of eternity . . . whatever *that* really meant.

She shuffled towards the door of the pub in her flat-soled, black shoes—the shoes she used for going about every day, and which could certainly not compete with the lashings of high heel that her girlfriends utilised.

She made it outside without any of them calling out to her.

And she knew that they were already neck-deep in conversation with Leo once more.

That they had snapped him up like they had so many men before.

In a way, she felt a sort of pity for him, that he really hadn't much of an idea of just what he was getting himself in for . . . she hoped that the language barrier wouldn't mean that he couldn't defend himself . . . well, he'd done just fine for himself back at the library with her earlier on in the day . . .

As Sophia padded along the cobbled streets, hardly another soul about now since it was nearing about ten thirty at night, she felt the breeze blowing against her cheeks, bringing them to life with that chill as much as it brought her skin out into puckered pimples.

The orange juice which she had nursed all night long now tasted somehow flat, and bitter on her tongue, and she was looking forwards to fixing herself a warming cup of hot chocolate to get herself rid of it . . . and to get her mind off Leo, and what her girl-friends might do to him.

It had been too good to be true after all.

Hadn't that been the story of her life thus far?

It was as she strode on harder, feeling the slight burn at the backs of her saggy-fleshed calves, that she heard the voice. The *familiar* voice calling out to her.

She couldn't quite believe it.

Couldn't really *bring* herself to believe it.

Because, when she looked back, there he was.

Leo.

Still sticking one of his arms into the leather jacket he'd hastily thrown about his shoulders. He looked concerned. His face alive with wrinkles, frown lines. And she realised that he was a good ten years older than her, though surely she had registered that before?

As he walked towards her, she could feel her heart welling in her throat, and her chest tightening. Because this had to be a dream. There was *no way* that this *couldn't* be a dream.

At one point she'd studied something about quantum physics—where she'd learned about multiple worlds, infinite possibilities . . .

had that been quantum physics or something else . . . some other subject . . . but she couldn't have foreseen this.

Hadn't he *seen* Elena, or Alexa . . . *Terri* if he was so into his blondes?

But he was here. With her.

Striding towards her with a look of concern on his face.

It was only when he took those final steps that Sophia thought to really—*truly*—believe that this was happening.

She felt his glow—the warmth still clinging to him from the pub.

And she breathed him in.

That rugged odour of cologne, and musk, and—well—was that what *muscles* smelled like?

She caught those silver eyes in her own, saw the way they caught fire in the orange glow from the streetlights, and before she really knew what was happening, he was sucking her into him. Into his chest. Into his *strong* chest. And pressing his lips up against hers.

His beard scratched her cheeks just a little.

But the sensation sent shimmers across the surface of her skin.

Made it seem like her blood was tingling.

Her heart pounded in her throat.

They seemed to kiss for about ten minutes, or more, and when she broke away from him, when she drew back, she saw that his eyes were wide with wonder.

She couldn't quite believe this was taking place here—and *now*.

But it was.

When she opened her mouth to speak, he hushed her, reached out and placed his thick, sausage-like finger on the surface of her lips.

"You and me, we must love," he said.

As far as romantic proposals went, it was probably at least in the Top Ten—if not the Top Five—for Sophia . . . she guessed that she'd have to take it.

Only when they had kissed once more, and broken apart anew, did she think to look beyond Leo, and to the *Dummard's Yarn* where she observed Elena, Alexa and Terri all leaving—their bags of shopping dangling from their fingers.

She didn't call out to them—she had no reason to speak with them.

But she somewhat enjoyed watching their slightly drunken gait as they wandered on away from her, picking their way along the cobblestones.

She vaporised them from her mind—forgot them instantly—when she turned her attention back to Leo, and to his silvery eyes.

Because he was *hers*.

And he was now.

TOO SHORT, TOO TALL

PHILLIP JUMPED DOWN OFF THE BUS determined to get it over and done with. He meandered his way through the early morning shopping crowds and arrived outside the cafe.

A large purple sign hung above the door. Its letters were outlined in gold leaf and had been freshly painted. On the other side of the window Phillip's girlfriend, Tracy, hunched over a table blowing the foam off her cappuccino.

He took a deep breath and shoved the door open. Somewhere inside a bell tinkled to itself. He took in the room, actively trying to keep his eyes off Tracy, pretending he hadn't already seen her.

She called to him. "Philly? Philly?"

Blood twitched threw his veins. Slowly, he turned his head to face her. He tried his best to put on a smile, but it dwindled and ended as something more of a grimace.

She beamed in his direction.

He seemed to drift over to the table. Floorboards creaked under his feet and he hovered near the seat.

"Are you going to sit then?" she said.

God should he do it now? There didn't seem much point in him beating about the bush, buying a coffee. He coughed then glanced down at the chair opposite. "Er, erm, okay." He sat.

Her blue eyes sparkled and her cropped hair sauntered about her eyes when she sipped her coffee. She dabbed her lips with a napkin then leaned across the table and planted a kiss on his lips. Backing up, she said, "What's this about?"

"Well, it's just something tha—"

"Aren't you getting a coffee?"

It would be pretty heartless just to turn up and dump her. Perhaps he could just have one coffee then stop her if she went to buy another. Girls cried when they got dumped, they liked to make a scene. Things would only be worse if she bought a coffee she couldn't finish.

He scratched the back of his neck and rose from his seat. "You want anything?"

"Nah, I'm okay," she said.

He nodded then strolled up to the counter where he ordered the cheapest coffee going. On second thought, he bent over and laid a muffin on the counter too. Girls liked chocolate.

Back at the table, he laid the muffin down.

Her eyes rounded, she reached out then peeled off the plastic. She broke off a piece and popped it into her mouth. "Yum," she said. "What's the special occasion? You never buy anything when we come here normally."

This was his chance. She knew something was up. It would only make things worse to talk about inanities. He had to bite his lip and get the deed done. He shifted in his seat then glanced down at his black coffee. "All right, I asked you to come here today because we have to talk."

Her brow furrowed.

"It's about you and me. I don't think it's working."

"What're you talking about?"

He leaned in closer. "Things haven't been good for the last few weeks, you know that."

Her lips parted slightly and her eyes drifted onto his then drifted away again. She pinched her lips together, puffed out her cheeks then grinned.

Sparks danced down his spine. This wasn't how it was supposed to be. She should be in tears right now. He backed up into his seat. "You're okay with it then?"

"Yeah, well, I'm glad that one of us had a chance to say it."

His chest still felt numb. Maybe she was in shock. He gritted his teeth. "Do you want to know why?"

She licked her lips and drew in her smile. "Does it really matter?"

Heat rose in his cheeks. Didn't their relationship mean anything to her? The way she was acting all pointed to one thing: she was seeing another guy. He narrowed his eyes. "It might be useful for the future."

She shrugged.

"It's just, you're so small," he said.

She cocked her pretty blond head to one side and stared at him. Her fist grasped her mug, turning her knuckles white.

This was better. Some emotion was better than no emotion, even if it was anger. The most important thing was to get everything out on the table, leave no loose ends.

"And what's your problem with my size?" she said.

He tightened his mouth. "It's difficult for us walking down the street. It just doesn't look right. Something from the circus."

"What about you?"

"Me?"

"Yeah, maybe it's that you're too tall."

"What're you talking about?"

"It might be your problem. You've grown too much. I mean, look around. There aren't many people who're approaching seven foot."

His brain pulsed in his skull. He realised he was getting angry. This wasn't the plan at all. "That's ridiculous," he said.

"Why?"

"Well, it's—"

"You don't fit through doors, you have to get clothes specially made and you don't fit in cars."

"But I take the bus usually."

"Remember when we went up to my parents' cottage?"

"Yeah."

"Don't you remember all that mucking about to get you into the seat? Then you snapped the door frame getting out."

"Well, I needed something to hold onto. Not easy to get your legs in the right place."

"There we go then. It's got nothing to do with my size. Then what's this about?"

Why was this getting so difficult? All he wanted was for them to go their separate ways. She'd always been too bright for him. She could talk the spots off a leopard.

He rubbed his temples. Remembering his cup of coffee, he reached down then brought it up to his lips. He replaced it on its ring. "Maybe it's that we're just not right for one another."

"I think we're as right as two people can be for one another."

"Right."

"I mean, the whole point of a relationship is to work together on making it better. We have to be patient."

This wasn't going right. He had hoped getting personal, picking out her physical details, would make things move much quicker. One more go might work. He knocked back the rest of his coffee. "I can do better than you."

She snorted. "Unlikely."

"What makes you so sure?"

"Someone like you? A gawky, oafish, clumsy idiot?"

"Wha—?"

"Trust me, for you, I'm a catch."

A strange tingling feeling draped over him. He'd never been the most confident of guys and he'd always thought about his height giving him an advantage over other men—that was what his mum had always told him anyway. He played with his coffee spoon.

"Convinced?" she said.

Why couldn't she have been like other girls, the ones he saw on TV? He looked about the cafe. "Uh—"

"Good, because I wanted to talk about starting a family."

"Really?"

"Yes. Any objections?"

This might be his last opportunity. "I don't want kids."

"Don't be silly," she said. "Everyone says that then when they arrive, it's all fine."

"Uh, okay."

She smiled and reached behind her for her jacket. "Everything all right, then?"

He rose and glanced about.

"Well?"

"Yeah, I think so," he said.

She sidled up beside him and crooked her arm through his. "Let's go then. There's some baby shopping to get done."

He took a final glance about the cafe and tried to find a way out, but there was nowhere else to go. He let out a quiet sigh then allowed her to lead him out into the street.

PLAYGROUND

FOAM OVERFLOWED the washing up bowl and hot water steamed up the windows.

Lizzy snatched up another plate and scrubbed off the ketchup and butter stains. A bead of sweat rolled down her cheek. She wiped it off with the back of her hand.

She dropped a plate on the drying rack with a *thud-clunk* and wiped her soapy hands on her jeans.

It was best to do the dishes around this time, after dinner when kids went out for the quick play before bedtime.

That way she could supervise Graham without letting him know she was watching.

She wiped away a circle of condensation on the windowpane and peered out, trying to locate him. Footballs bounced, girls skipped rope, older kids flopped over bikes or fell off skateboards.

No sign of Graham.

A sharp pain stabbed her skull and a bout of dizziness caught her. She sucked in air and placed her hands on either side of the sink to steady herself.

Her husband, Alexander, cleared his throat and rustled his newspaper. His shoes and suit jacket lay in a heap at his feet. He shifted in his chair, causing it to squeak.

She gritted her teeth and fought the pain. ". . . F—fancy a cup of tea?"

"All right," Alexander said, without looking up.

She plucked the kettle off its base, filled it with water then replaced it. For a few seconds she lingered at the window, still unable to see Graham. "Might go and check on Gray. See what he's up to."

"Suit yourself."

Despite being summer, it kicked up a fierce chill in the

evenings, so she threw a fleece around her shoulders. She shoved open the wooden front door, allowing it to bounce off its rubber stop.

An elderly lady, Mrs Smith, rolled a bag of groceries through the hallway. She smiled at Lizzy and continued up the steps. Muted gunshots and screams floated down the stairwell.

Kids playing a videogame.

Lizzy arrived outside the block and glanced around. A group of girls sat at one corner of the muddy patch of grass with a small table between them and dolls in their laps. The dresses, those of the girls and the dolls, were caked in mud. A football skidded toward her and slapped into the brick wall, inches below her window.

One of the boys slid past her and retrieved it.

It was Thomas or 'Smelly', as she called him, though not to his face.

Like always, sweat pooled in the pits of his t-shirt and his hair was plastered to his forehead. He dropkicked the ball back into play. She collared him before he could return to the game. "Seen Graham about?"

Smelly looked her up and down then attempted to wriggle from her grasp, but she held firm. He scowled. "Round back with Winshaw's lot, innie?"

She released him and he skittered back onto the pitch.

If she'd told Graham once, she'd told him a thousand times to stay away from Winshaw.

She marched off around the corner.

It was difficult to miss Winshaw. He was thirteen and a smudge over six foot. He wore a black hoodie, like always, and loomed over a group of half a dozen other boys. All of them were a good foot smaller and five or six years younger. Winshaw's diamond earring glinted through his stringy blond hair in the fading sunlight.

Shouts and screams reverberated around the circle and Winshaw took something in his hand. She caught a flash of green before Winshaw knocked his head back and brought whatever was in his hand to his mouth.

The boys around him burbled with excitement.

She spotted Graham standing on the edge. He wasn't joining in with the others. His mouth was straight and his eyes sunken in their sockets. He gripped his trouser pockets tight, like he always did when he was nervous.

A hot feeling rushed through her. She gritted her teeth and trotted up to the group. Once she got close, she noticed the tin of green paint, discarded on the grass beside them.

Graham's mouse, Scuttly, peered out from inside Winshaw's wide-open mouth.

Green paint trickled from Winshaw's lips and onto his chin.

The boy was manic. Nonetheless, the key was to remain calm, not to get angry. Otherwise he would get the upper hand. She pushed through a pair of boys and confronted him. She kept her lips thin, face serious and held out her hand. "Spit him out."

Winshaw threw up his hands and spun about on the spot. His long hair wheeled about with him. He stopped, leant forward then spat Scuttly into her hand.

Scuttly shook himself off then curled up into a ball in her palm. She snatched Graham by his shirt sleeve and led him away from the group. "Come on."

"Mummy come to help you?" Winshaw said in a reedy voice.

The boys all laughed.

Graham allowed her to lead him away. He took two steps for each of hers.

"Do you want to go out with me, Mrs Gibson?" Windshaw called after her.

Another long round of laughter.

There was no point rising to the bait.

Idiots like Winshaw were a fact of life around here. She kept walking and finally turned the corner, keeping a firm grip on Scuttly till they got back to their block. She pushed back into the flat and let go of Graham with a sigh. "Get Daddy to run you a bath."

Graham pulled off his shoes and crossed the sitting room.

Alexander rolled his shoulders, curled his paper into a funnel then stuck it down the crack in the chair. He shot a glance at the green mouse in Lizzy's hand then followed Graham toward the bathroom.

Hands shaking, she carried Scuttly over to the sink and plonked him down. She ran a stream of water, mixing the cold with the hot until it was warm. "Let's get you washed."

Scuttly twitched under the water, his fur shimmering.

"It's okay, I know it's a bit undignified, but we can't have you looking like a minor nuclear accident, can we?"

Scuttly sneezed.

After ten minutes of washing, she'd got most of the paint out of Scuttly's fur. A tinge of green remained, but there wasn't much hope of getting that out—unless she put him in a sixty degree cycle.

She carried him through the flat and into Graham's room. There was a wire cage on the windowsill. She placed Scuttly inside and shut the latch.

Muffled voices and the occasional splash came from the bathroom. She stood and listened. Those were calming sounds, the sounds that made her feel at home. Warmth passed through her, but she resisted the urge to smile. It made her angry that she was always the big bad mummy, when Alexander got to be the cool dad.

Then she moved onto the real issue.

How to keep Graham out of the clutches of Winshaw.

Once they'd got Graham to bed, Lizzy sat with Alexander in

the sitting room. She picked up a pair of Graham's trousers, sewing up a tear in one of the knees, while Alexander bashed away at his Sudoku. The flat was silent. Only the odd screech and titter of laughter broke the tranquillity.

The teenagers mucking about outside.

Lizzy put her sewing onto the arm of the sofa and inspected her work. "Graham was round back with Winshaw again."

"Was he?"

"It's not normal."

Alexander squinted at his paper. "How old's Winshaw? Ten, eleven?"

"Thirteen."

"Really?"

"Yes."

"And what should we do about it?"

"Don't know. It'd seem cruel to keep Graham locked up. But I don't want him running around the back where I can't see him."

"Yeah."

She sucked her bottom lip and looked out of the window, to the play area.

Floodlights beamed an even glow over the outside.

She had to do something.

"Alex?" she said.

"Yeah?"

"Do you think someone should sort out a playground there? Something fenced off. For the younger kids, I mean. I'd be able to see him right out of the kitchen window. There's not much about here for kids of Gray's age and if we get one built we can tell him to stick to it.

If he wanders out, I'll haul him right back inside."

Alexander stuck out his tongue and scratched out something on his Sudoku. "Sounds good to me."

"I'll look into it, then."

"What about the other kids?"

"What do you mean?"

"You know, the teenagers. Won't they smash it into kingdom come?"

Lizzy opened and closed a fist. "Not if there's someone watching them, they won't."

Alexander slapped his paper down. He stood and stretched, sucking in a yawn. "That's me done for today. You coming to bed?"

"In a bit."

He leant over and kissed her on the forehead. She hated it when he did that. It made her feel like she was his sister, or mother. "Don't stay up mangling your brains too long," he said, "might mess with your good looks." He patted her on the bottom and left.

Lizzy got up and rested her hands on the edge of the kitchen sink, looking out over the play area.

That great big muddy patch.

There must've been hundreds of kids living in the blocks of flats. Why hadn't anyone ever thought to build a playground?

She scrubbed away the last of the green paint at the bottom of the sink then headed off to bed where Alexander lay on his side, facing the wall. For a long time she lay on her back staring at the ceiling, listening to teenagers lurking outside.

In the morning, she got up before Alexander or Graham and went about getting breakfast ready.

She peered out across the play area in the early morning sun.

Dew glistened on the remaining patches of grass, while the sun peeped out between the opposite blocks of flats.

Once she'd got Alexander and Graham fed, off to work and

school, she left the plates drying, fed Scuttly and headed out to take a better look. She walked across the surface.

Footprints, bike tracks and dog shit punctuated mud and tufts of grass.

It would take a bit of work to get it in a good state.

And she wouldn't be able to do it alone. She needed help. Money.

At the other end of the strip, she took in the whole area, trying to envision what she'd put up. A slide, jungle gym—perhaps a basketball hoop—a couple of goal posts so the kids could play football without getting their jumpers dirty. Then maybe a—

"Good morning, Mrs Gibson."

Lizzy flinched and looked around.

Winshaw stood, hands on hips, in his school uniform. His tie dangled over the fringe of his untucked shirt.

Why couldn't the boy just disappear? She pressed a finger to her temple. "Go to school."

With the same smile, Winshaw cocked his head. "What about you? Aren't you going to work?"

She kept her eyes fixed on his.

"Dad says you're too lazy to work."

Her brain fizzed with obscenities, but she kept her lips pressed tight. No way would he get a rise out of her. He was just an obnoxious teenager. She'd heard it all before.

Her illness was nothing to be ashamed of.

Winshaw batted his fringe from his eye. "What're you doing out here, anyway? Shouldn't you be in bed?"

"Actually, I'm thinking about redoing this area. Fixing things up for our kids."

He pouted. "But I like it the way it is."

"You would. It's not *for* you anyway."

"Have you thought about my offer?"

"What're you talking about?"

He winked then his smile weakened a fraction. "Don't you want to be my girlfriend?"

"Buzz off."

His nimble fingers wandered up the strap of his school bag. He caught her eye then flicked his hair and trudged off.

Didn't his parents care that he got to school late every day? Some people just weren't up to having kids. She'd often thought it would be a good idea to force prospective parents into taking an exam before having kids.

Come the revolution.

She returned to her flat, pulled a leaf of paper from the printer and set it on the table with a pencil in hand. Then, with a ruler, she drew out a rectangle. The play area. She sketched a zone for the playground and, alongside, a smaller space for a micro football pitch.

Her chest hummed. If she managed to get this thing off the ground, not only Graham but all the kids in the block of flats would have somewhere to play. Somewhere safe. The fact that each flat looked out onto the play area meant families could watch their children playing. She hoped it would drive out the older kids, Winshaw.

There wasn't much interesting about a supervised playground to a teenager.

At late morning she knocked back a cup of coffee and headed out to bounce her idea off her neighbour, Alisha.

Hopefully she would be sympathetic, being a parent herself. She rang the bell and waited.

There was a scuffling within then Alisha emerged, dressed in her tracksuit, hair half straightened. She had a thick Jamaican accent. "What's goin' on?"

"I've been thinking about your Manny and my Graham, I want to build a playground."

"And what d'you wan' from me?"

"Thought you might want to help out."

Alisha pouted then shrugged. "Bit busy today. I gotta go ta work."

Lizzy glanced around her into the flat.

A TV blabbered on while dirty plates and cups littered the sitting room, covering the coffee table and carpet.

Lizzy grinned and said, "Not right now. I guess there's stuff to do first. You know, getting permission, and all that."

Alisha shifted her weight from one foot to the other. "How're ya goin' ta raise the money?"

"Haven't thought about it."

"Going ta cost a lot, I reckon."

"But you'd help out?"

Alisha flashed her eyes and glanced backed into her flat. "Look, I don' have money ta give, if tha's what you think."

"I just wanted your opinion."

Alisha pursed her lips. "I'll think abou' it."

"Great."

Alisha slunk back inside and clicked the door shut.

Well, Lizzy hadn't expected a glowing reception. At least Alisha had a vague interest. That was all the validation she needed, just to know she wasn't crazy. She returned to her flat and logged herself onto the computer.

In between loads of washing, Lizzy searched through online catalogues, marking out what she needed and the prices. Once done, she investigated how they'd go about getting the right surfaces.

She sent off emails to various members of the council, sounding out the feasibility of her proposal. Around a quarter to three, leaving to go and pick up Graham, she received a reply from a councillor's secretary asking her to call back tomorrow morning for a chat.

Her bones and muscles felt light as she marched off to the school.

That evening, after Graham had gone to bed, she sat in the sitting room.

Alexander sat reading the sports pages, his feet hanging over the arm of the chair while she looked back through her plans for the playground, typing them up—chopping and changing.

"What're you beavering away at there?" Alexander said.

She minimised the window and glanced over the laptop screen. "Putting together a package on the new playground."

"Moved that fast, has it?"

"Yeah, I'm calling the council tomorrow."

He looked back at his paper then clucked his tongue.

Whenever he made that sound it meant he was mulling something over. "What's the matter?" she said.

He finished his sentence then glanced up. "It's just, I was thinking about something today."

"What?"

"Well, you know, it might be better if we moved away from here. Found a better place. Doesn't make sense putting all your energy into this place. It'll just spit back at you."

They'd had this conversation a thousand times before and it always reached the same dead end. "We don't have the money," she said. "Don't you remember how long it took us to find this flat? Somewhere this cheap doesn't come around every day."

He shifted, adjusted the lay of his trouser crease. "I was thinking about that too."

"And?"

"You seem to be doing much better. Perhaps you could get back to work."

His voice seemed far away, muffled. People around her, tapping away. Phones ringing. Bosses shouting. She felt her body sinking into her chair. A nausea seized her and she had to steady herself with the table. Her brain spiralled out of control, like spinning on a roundabout, carving its way into the earth. "I—I'm sorry." She swallowed then gasped air. "I jus—just can't."

He got up and came over, wrapped his arms about her. His touch assured her. "Sorry, love," he said. "I didn't mean to set you off."

Her hands shook. It was so frustrating that she could be completely fine one moment then as soon as the stresses and rigors of work came back to her, she dwindled into despair. She tried to think of the words but realised it was impossible to explain.

It was just a profound emptiness.

He squeezed her hand and rose. "Let's get you a glass of water. Put you to bed. You've gone all pale."

She allowed him to take her to their bedroom. He laid her down and brought the blanket up to her chin. He sat on the end of the bed, his breathing heavy and regular, staring at some point in the middle distance, at the light spilling in from the corridor.

When the world spun a little less, Lizzy set her head down on the pillow.

The next morning, Lizzy sat at the phone trying to get herself ready for the call. She rattled her bottle and shook out a pill. Its chemical yellow ran into her pale skin. She knocked it back and swallowed without water. After another five minutes or so she got her head together. She picked the phone off its cradle and held it to her ear, listening to the dial tone buzzing away. Her trembling subsided and she entered the numbers for the council office. There was a click on the other end. "Hardacre Council. How can I help?"

"Oh, hello," Lizzy said, "this is Elizabeth Gibson. I'm calling about a playground at the flats."

There was a scrunching of paper and a scrabbling of keyboard. "One moment, Mrs Gibson."

Lizzy drummed her fingers against the desk. A reflex she'd picked up from her grandfather, a piano player. One of his loosening exercises.

"Mrs Gibson?"

"Yes."

"I'm going to put you through to Mr Henry Wilcox, who's in charge of Community Development."

"Thanks."

Another dial tone then Wilcox answered. She went through her details and the plan she'd outlined. Once she'd finished, she could hardly breathe. She cast her mind back to her doctor's advice—to stay away from stressful situations.

This was about Graham, though.

Feeling somewhat exasperated from explaining it all, she caught her breath and then said, to Wilcox, "So, what do you think?"

Wilcox sounded a long way away, like she'd caught him off guard. "It's a little more complicated than that."

Her heart hammered. "What do you mean?"

"There's lots paperwork, applications for permission, that sort of thing."

A knot formed in her throat and her palms sweated. She blacked out for a couple of moments.

". . . Mrs Gibson? Mrs Gibson?"

She snapped back to the present, the insistence in his voice awakening her. "Yes," she said, "I'm still here."

"Do you understand? It's better that you leave this for now. If you submit a proposal for the playground, we may be able to put you on the waiting list."

"How long would that be?"

"Oh, I couldn't say. Somewhere between eighteen months and three, four years. We're very busy, you see?"

Pain stabbed her right between the eyes and she got dizzy. ". . . No," she said in a husky voice, almost a whisper.

"Sorry?"

"No, we don't have time."

He chuckled. "I'm afraid there's very little I can do. We have to follow the process."

A tremor passed through her skull and she almost lost her hold of the handset. All the energy was sapped from her body.

"Mrs Gibson?"

She sensed the impatience in his voice. That same thinly veiled anger which she noted in the voice of everyone who had worked in her office. She massaged her neck. "Yes. I understand."

"Good," he said, before adding, "thank you for calling."

He hung up.

It felt like her brain was expanding and contracting, like a sponge. She replaced the phone then stumbled to the kitchen sink and poured herself a glass of water, all the time telling herself she was okay. But the pain kept coming back.

She headed to the bedroom for a lie down.

Once she got over the dizzy spell she decided the playground had to happen, no matter what stood in her way. Money and help was what she needed.

She got up out of bed, grabbed her coat and did the rounds of the flats.

Most people answered their doors and listened to what she said. She learnt that it helped to keep talking at people until they committed money to the project in an effort to fob her off.

When the questions about permission and the council came around, she avoided them as best she could. By the end of an afternoon's work, she had got a list of names.

Enough committed cash to get work started in any case.

The weeks shot by and the materials arrived, one by one, at her door. She got to be on first name terms with the delivery man and he kept up a running joke about her building a shelter for a coming storm.

Soon she had all the materials ready to put into the playground. It was just a question of putting it all together, like doing a life-size puzzle.

Delighted to have the materials together, she called on Alisha. "It's all ready to go up."

Today Alisha was dressed in a pair of dungarees.

The cardboard boxes, bags full of cement and wood chippings, were all stacked up in the stairwell.

Alisha whistled. "And where d'ya get all the money for this?"

"People in the flats."

"Dishin' it out, are they?"

She shot Alisha a glance. "Most people gave something."

"What abou' the play equipment? The slide?"

"I'm keeping it in my flat, in the front room."

"Mus' be takin' up a lotta space."

Lizzy brushed some dust from one of the boxes. It made her cough. "It's only for a little while."

Alisha rolled her eyes but nodded her head.

"I'm going round, asking people to help out."

"I have ta work. I don' have time for this."

Lizzy thought about protesting but she consoled herself with the fact that Alisha wasn't actively opposing her. After all, if she wanted, she could file a report to the council.

Enlisting help from a few contractors about the complex, a

group of out-of-work fathers, Lizzy oversaw the digging. It took several weeks and an excavator.

Where the excavator came from, she had no idea.

In the meantime, her whole body filled with worry. Every sound in the middle of the night woke her. What if someone came along and told them to stop?

On the day the excavating was finished, she glanced at her watch. She was appalled to see Graham had been out of school for five minutes already.

She rushed off to school with images of older kids throwing him about over their heads. When she got there, however, he sat alone on the wall, kicking the scuffed-up heels of his school shoes against the bricks as if he would wait there forever out of pure faith.

She bent down, kissed him on the cheek then took him by the hand and led him home.

They sat down to dinner, a frozen lasagne she had stuck in the oven. She dished out the plates and allowed herself to relax. Although she had her worries, the project had filled her with a sense of purpose and she smiled at the prospect of throwing herself into it again tomorrow.

Alexander took two mouthfuls and then half a glass of water to counter the baking hot lasagne. He jerked his head back to indicate the play area. "That's a dirty great mess out there."

"Yeah, the cement's all ready to go in tomorrow. It's going to look quite different."

Graham chewed with his mouth open. "What're you building, Mummy?"

"A playground. For you and your friends."

"What? Like Winshaw?"

Lizzy screwed up her eyes. "No. Your *friends*."

Graham cast a glance at Alexander.

Alexander munched through his current mouthful. "You

know"—he twirled his fork—

"T—uh, Tom—Thomas. He's your friend, isn't he?"

"He's boring," Graham said. "Smells of farts. Don't really like him."

Thinking of Smelly, her name for him, Lizzy restrained a chuckle. "Of course you *like* him, you invited him to your birthday party last year, remember?"

Graham shrugged.

Alexander exchanged glances with her.

Lizzy said, "Once we've got this playground built it's going to be just for you and boys your own age. Won't it be nice that the others will go play somewhere else? You'll have a space just for you. And I'll be able to see you. No more running off round back."

Graham chewed his lasagne, gulped it down then said, "I like Winshaw. He's my friend."

"No," Lizzy said, "Winshaw is a bully. He doesn't do things that make you feel nice, does he? He just makes fun of you and your things because it makes the other boys laugh."

"I like him. He's cool."

Her blood bubbled. "*No*, he's *not*. Boys like Winshaw are what's wrong with places like this."

"Places like what?" Graham said.

She sighed. "Let's just eat our dinner in peace and quiet."

The room filled with the sounds of cutlery clinking on plates. Then there was a commotion outside, shouts and screams. She perked up and looked out the window.

A group of boys of varying ages, led by Winshaw, bounded across the play area, toward the hole the excavator had dug out. They slipped under the yellow tape the men had put up, then slid down the sides, pulling mud back into the pit. She laid her knife and fork down at the side of her plate and tried to ward off the tightness in her lungs.

Alexander glanced over his shoulder and sighed. "Bloody kids.

Never give it a rest, do they?"

Graham got up from his seat and peered out. He cocked his head to her. "Can I go out for a bit?"

"No, it's bath time," Lizzy said, her eyes still on Winshaw.

"Aw," Graham said, slinking away from the table.

She calmed herself. There wasn't much point her getting angry. It would just tire her out. She reassured herself it wasn't an unsolvable problem.

Just half an hour to clear it up tomorrow.

After she'd cleaned up the plates, and the screams and shouts had quietened down, she went outside to inspect the hole.

It looked like an earthquake had hit it.

She stared at the trampled sides and debris sitting at the bottom.

"This is what you get."

Her spine tingled. A flash of fear. She glanced up to see Winshaw. "Shouldn't you be inside, having your tea?"

Winshaw inspected his blackened fingernails. "Nah, I'll heat up some chips in the microwave later."

"Where're your parents?"

"Working."

A shred of sympathy hit her. She tried her best to ward it off, but it wouldn't go away. What chance did the kid have when his parents were never around?

Her entire body and soul warned her, but she knew she couldn't give up on a kid in need. "Come with me."

He held back, the same stupid grin on his face. "You're just going to lure me to your lair. Rape me. Something like that."

Her heart leapt into her throat. Every word was an invitation for her to lose control. But, against all odds, she held on. "I've got some lasagne left over." She continued on her way, back toward the flat. When she looked over her shoulder, she saw he was following. They reached the door. "Wait here."

He did as he was told.

She returned with a plate and handed it to him. His eyes widened and he took the fork from her and polished off the plate in under a minute. "Want some more?" she said.

He nodded.

Once he'd finished the second plate, she took it off him. "Off you go, then."

Winshaw surveyed her a moment then grinned. Still smiling, he traipsed off across the muddy grass and headed in through the main door of building C. She watched him all the way then took one look at the hole and returned inside.

The next day, she helped the workmen undo Winshaw's damage. Then they worked on the foundations amongst a host of other technicalities which Lizzy didn't even attempt to understand.

The men, like her, seemed glad to have something to do.

Around lunchtime, Alisha strolled out and looked over the work.

"What do you think?" Lizzy said.

"No' bad."

Coming from Alisha, she supposed she should take that as a compliment. She smiled and took another look at their work, a warm glow filling her.

At dinner, she forced herself to calm down, to stop glancing out the window every moment at the drying cement. It would be like a magnet for Winshaw. How could he resist? Indeed, later on that night, while relaxing in the sitting room, she heard Winshaw's half broken voice rallying his troops.

She rose and pulled back the curtain, gazing out across the floodlit area. Smelly—Thomas—danced out across the battered turf heading for the new cement. No doubt wanting to scribble something obscene on the kids' playground.

Her breath hitched in her throat.

She readied herself for a battle.

Winshaw shouted something across the area.

The boy slowed his pace.

Winshaw shouted again.

The boy stopped dead in his tracks.

Lizzy's heart skipped a beat.

What was going on?

With a shrug, the boy turned right around and dashed off in the opposite direction. She caught Winshaw's eye for a second. His face was calm and eyes sunk back in their sockets. Then he winked, smiled and spun around, chasing after the boy.

She shuddered and turned back into the sitting room.

Alexander peeped over his paper. "Everything all right?"

Tiredness crept over her and she could barely keep her eyes open. She sank down into the armchair. "Yeah, fine."

"Not messing about with the playground, are they?"

"No."

He rustled his paper. "That's good. Let me know if they do and I'll go out there and have words."

A numbness seeped into her muscles, worked its way into her bones. Of course he would, if he could manage to escape the arse groove he'd worked into the sofa cushion. "Thanks."

Over the next few days, she enlisted the help of others in the block of flats. They got everything together and the playground was ready. Although she felt the same uneasiness at night, Winshaw, and his merry band of young idiots, never returned to wreak havoc.

In the late evening light, she stood with her hands on hips and examined their work.

A playground had sprung up out of mud and turf.

There was a slide and a set of swings, half a dozen of them either side. A roundabout stood primed and ready. At the other end there was a climbing wall. Alongside the playground the football pitch had been marked out, a pair of goals with crisp white nets billowing in the breeze.

She steeled herself and tried to make herself believe it was real.

Tomorrow afternoon they would have an official opening.

The kids would play on it.

They had somewhere to go now— bureaucracy be damned.

That night, she tossed and turned, and before she could quite absorb the fact, it was the next day.

She got up at first light, washed and dressed, then stood out to see the playground in the sunrise.

Her heart fluttered and she could hardly contain her excitement.

First, she headed off to the shops and got some bottles of bubbly, along with a few sets of disposable glasses. Then she came back to bake a large cake. Every few moments, she'd glance out the window at her creation, still unable to quite believe it was there.

She went around the flats and solicited chairs and tables from each.

Around three o'clock, the first kids were drifting back home from school. She headed out to pick up Graham, her mind flying through a thousand ideas a second.

She returned with Graham and got him to help her put the final touches to the ceremony.

Together they dragged a red ribbon around the playground and set out the napkins, resting pebbles on top to keep them blowing away in the wind.

There was still no sign of Winshaw, but that didn't mean Lizzy had forgotten him.

Alexander sidled up to her. "Are you going to cut the ribbon?"

She hadn't thought about who would cut it. She'd put it up on autopilot. It had seemed the thing to do. "Me?"

He shrugged and knocked back his glass.

"Well, okay."

A pair of shears stood ready on a nearby table. She set her glass down, exchanging it for the shears. Someone rattled a spoon against a glass and a hush fell over the group. Her mind bolted about, thinking that Winshaw might strike at any moment.

This would be his perfect stage.

Everything had led up to this.

She clutched the shears in her clammy hands, snapped open the blades then brought them shut with a *swoosh*.

The ribbon crumpled to the ground and the crowd let out a cheer.

Children poured onto the playground, taking up places on the swings or fighting to get up into the jungle gym and onto the slide. The burble of children's laughter reverberated against the block of flats and for the first time she truly felt at home.

Alisha strolled into the area, still in her work clothes. There was a man at her heels. He wore a grey suit and carried a briefcase. His expression was stern, business-like.

For a second, she smiled at him, hoping to bust a crack in his otherwise unfeeling façade.

And then it struck her.

It was everything she had feared.

Her whole body seemed to shut down.

But, somehow, she kept it together and didn't faint.

The man approached her and held out his hand.

She shook it.

"Name's Brian Wilcox," he said, "I work with the council, I believe we spoke on the telephone." He brought his briefcase up into his arms, flipped it open and slid out a document. "We are charging you with illegally putting up this playground on public property."

Her entire body froze over.

How could Alisha do this to her?

After all she had gone through, the trouble the community had gone to, in getting the playground built.

She accepted the document.

Wilcox headed over to the playground and said in a loud voice to the kids, "All right, you lot, get off. We're closing this down. Health and safety."

The children let out a long and sustained, "Aw!"

None of them moved from their places.

Wilcox set his briefcase at his feet and clapped his hands. "Come on."

There had to be something they could do, some kind of arrangement.

Her skull squeezed her brain, dousing it in pain.

She snatched up a bottle of champagne, and a spare glass, then paced over to Mr Wilcox. His gaze shifted from the playground to her, then the bottle. She smiled. "Don't you have time for a quick drink?"

The intensity faded from him.

Alisha stepped in. "What's the matter here? Aren't you going to shut this down."

Ignoring her, Lizzy poured out a glass and held it to Wilcox, who, at first, waved it away. Then, when she insisted, he accepted it but didn't drink. He just stared down into the churning bubbles.

She took a deep breath and prepared her speech. "Look at all the work we've put in. Okay, I admit we didn't go through the right channels, but couldn't you arrange to get your people to look it over? Check it's safe?"

"Impossible," he said.

Tears pricked the corners of Lizzy's eyes. Her vision blurred and a huskiness crept into her voice. "But it's *here*."

He shook his head and handed back his glass of champagne. "I'm sorry, Mrs Gibson, you've left us with no other choice."

There was a shout, somewhere on the other side of the play area. She cast her eyes across the playground. It was Winshaw. He was running toward them. When he drew closer, she noticed he was crying. Her heart sank.

Winshaw ran up to Wilcox and pressed his hands to his chest.

Wilcox stepped back and waved his hands, as if trying to evade a fly.

Winshaw bawled, "Don't take this away! It's ours. You can't!"

His voice reached a higher pitch than Lizzy had ever heard.

It jangled her nerves.

Wilcox began to protest, "Pl—please, I'm just doing my job—"

Winshaw screamed louder and louder, stamping his feet. The kids on the playground, Graham among them, joined in. A wall of noise deafened her.

It ripped up her nerves and made her want to scream too.

Wilcox's eyes darted around, like a frightened animal.

Alisha grimaced and reached out for his arm, taking hold of it and guiding him back, away from the playground.

In the midst of the disorder, Winshaw shot Lizzy a wink.

Her insides tingled and her guts twisted.

She couldn't make sense of it.

Then she remembered the lasagne.

Was all this for a plate of lasagne?

She skipped after Wilcox and Alisha, keen to push her advantage. Over the uproar, she addressed Wilcox, "How about we go inside? I'm sure we can come to some agreement."

Wilcox's features creased and he nodded, over and over.

~

Over a cup of tea, they talked over the situation. Although Lizzy had glossed over the permission, not submitted paperwork and generally made life difficult for Wilcox, he agreed that there might be a way to sort out the playground—to make it legal—on condition that the parents kept their children away in the meantime.

Nonetheless, he made her agree to take responsibility for any injuries, in exchange for turning a blind eye, and warned of a lengthy process to get the whole situation sorted out.

Finally, Wilcox shook their hands and marched away from the block of flats, head bowed.

Over the passing weeks, she watched on, constantly running out and telling kids to get off the various pieces of equipment. Her heart leapt into her throat every time she saw a kid running for it.

Then, a few days later, Wilcox returned, with a pair of men dressed in overalls.

They spent most of the afternoon going over the playground, ticking off various items on their sheets. After they had finished, they knocked on her door and handed over a sheet which detailed the work required to make it safe.

She took it from them, already worried about how she might raise more money, then Wilcox stepped inside and handed her a cheque. He shook her hand, once again, and made her promise she wouldn't call the council again.

Everything passed off without a hitch and the playground was officially opened.

On a Saturday afternoon, she spread out a picnic blanket and settled down to watch the kids play.

She leant into Alexander and, for once, he put down his newspaper and embraced her.

Together they watched Graham laugh his way about the playground, up and down the slide, back and forth on the swings. And, for the first time in a long time, she felt totally calm and in control.

Like she could do anything.

MEDITERRANEAN ARMS

1

JOAN LAY BACK on the warmed-up beach towel. She could feel the gentle *creak* of the oak wood of the sun lounger beneath her. The sun was hot today, she could say that much, but, really, it was *hot* most days. She wouldn't have been able to wear anything more than a bikini even if she had been compelled to do so by the management.

She reached out to her side, now so aware of her surroundings that she didn't need to so much as glance, and felt the cool glass of fresh lemonade waiting for her there. She manoeuvred the plastic straw into the corner of her mouth and sucked back the chilly sweetness.

This really was paradise.

Or if it wasn't *quite* paradise, then it was at least close.

And close was good enough.

The air smelled lightly of almonds—the Mediterranean Arms Hotel's particular fragrance. In the near distance, she could hear the *slosh* of the waves as they rolled up on the shore. The *cackle* of sea birds.

There were summer jobs, and then there were *summer jobs,* and Joan couldn't quite believe that she had managed to land this one.

She replaced her lemonade back on the small table beside her, and then lay back on the lounger. She glanced down at herself, at her well-tanned body—even only after three days—and to the turquoise bikini she'd found hanging up on the doorknob of her room that morning. She got to keep all the bikinis she used throughout the day, and since this was the fourth day here, at the Mediterranean Arms, she was on her fourth bikini.

Her contract here would last for two months—almost the entire length of her summer holiday from university—so she wondered if she'd really manage to get her hands on fifty-six bikinis in the course of her holidays. More likely, there would be seven for her to wear throughout the summer and somebody would be along to launder them for her, one by one.

Though the pay was hardly magical here . . . or, for that matter *existent* there were other perks.

The free bikinis, of course, but then there was the free gym membership—though, really, that was a requirement. She had to keep herself 'toned-up', as the manager of the hotel had put it, so that she would 'drag the guests in with their tongues waggling out of their mouths'.

Then she had three free meals a day—though, not wanting to get herself fired, she only opted to take dinner—and the room itself, which, though it only had a view out onto the car park, was perfectly serviceable.

Yes, all things considered, this was gearing up to be the best summer job imaginable.

"Hey."

Joan held herself still on the sun lounger just for a couple of moments, before glancing up. She had learned all about the letches that hung about the beachfront here, where the Mediterranean Arms was situated. She could pretty much set her watch by them. Almost every quarter of an hour there was another. Some sad, old man stopping by to have a 'chat' with her. With his clumsy propositions: dinner that evening, a walk on the beach later, or a dip in the sea, perhaps?

What she told them, and what she was gearing up to tell *this* man, was that she spent all day on this sun lounger, lying in the sun, and though it might not look like hard work, there was certainly a toll which sunlight took on the mind after a while.

After a whole day of lying in the sun, she just wanted to take a shower and then lie in the dark of her bedroom for a little while.

That shook most of the men off.

And she was glad.

Joan drew in a deep breath, feeling her ribcage retract almost right down to her spine, and then she glanced to her side, where the voice had come from.

She already had a sharp riposte, just waiting on her tongue, but she found herself struck dumb almost right away. There, lying on the sun lounger beside her, was what must've been the perfect man —a man wearing nothing but Speedos, showing off his *extremely* well-kept body.

Sculptured body.

He looked a little pale to her, just like all the other new arrivals did, and she pretty much assumed that this was his first day here without him having to say so much.

The man met her eye, and Joan couldn't do much else than look right back at him. "They rope you into this too?" he said with a smile.

Joan smiled back at him. She tugged her sunglasses a little down her nose. "Yeah, all I really wanted was to go find a job in some department store back in Blighty, go out for lunchtime walks in the wind and the rain."

The man reached his hand out over to her. "Name's Monty," he said, "Pleased to meet you."

She accepted his handshake.

His skin was cool—*not* sweaty—and his shake was firm. She could smell a dab of his cologne over the almond odour of the hotel. Just for one dizzy moment—and maybe it was just the sun stroke talking—but she wondered just what that skin of his might taste like.

He broke off the handshake and, with a contented sigh, lay back on the lounger. "So," he said, "They recruited you back in the UK?"

"Yeah," she said.

He folded his hands back behind his head and closed his eyes, soaking up all the rays. "I was out here on the beach when Michael approached me."

Michael was the manager of the Mediterranean Arms, and though Joan had immediately pinned him as being lecherous—surely the sort of person who opened a hotel out here, on the Mediterranean Sea so that he might have the chance of shagging a few young hot things—she had been surprised to find that, thus far, he had been the perfect gentleman . . . though, looking over Monty here, she wondered if Michael might not be gay.

Michael was certainly something of a talent spotter.

"So," Monty continued, "What is it *exactly* that we have to do? I mean, on the beach, he told me that I get a free room out of the thing—*free food*—and all the Speedos that I could ever want."

Yeah, Joan had to admit that Michael, the manager of the hotel, was certainly tipping the scales towards the gay now . . .

Joan shrugged, which she soon realised wasn't all that easy while lying back on the sun lounger. "Just have to lie here, in the sun, so that we look good for any photographs people might take of the place. So that Michael can pick up on passing trade."

" 'Passing trade' ?" Monty said, with a slight splutter—only then did Joan realise that he'd taken a swig of his own lemonade while she'd been speaking—"You mean to say that there're people who show up here, to this resort, without having already booked a hotel?"

Joan cracked open an eye, catching the glistening ocean just over the tips of her toes. "The way I understand it, people can switch their booking with their tour operator during their holiday if they wish. They can switch for free to another hotel. So, the way I understand it, Michael wants people to walk past the façade here, see us"—she gestured to her chest—"and then immediately get in touch to change their booking."

"And Michael makes money out of that?" Monty asked.

"I guess he gets paid for the nights they stay here—on top of whatever they order out of the restaurant, or the bar . . . I guess some people want to use the gym too."

"And all that because there's a pair of people lying out here in the sun?"

Again, Joan shrugged. "From what I've seen these past few days, it seems to work. I've spotted several men—some of them with families—come past here and then, a few hours later, pop on in to change their booking to the Mediterranean Arms."

"Huh," Monty said, "Seems like you've got this whole thing worked out."

Joan smiled widely. "I'm a university girl—a fast learner."

They lay out there, being bleached in the sun for the rest of the afternoon. Neither of them spoke much after the initial flurry of conversation. There was just something about the sun which seemed to suck all the energy out of Joan, seemed to make even the simplest of tasks far harder. And so she just lay still, soaking it all up.

When the sun set on the horizon, Joan's cue for her to pack up shop for the day, she perched herself on the edge of her sun lounger and looked to Monty out of expectation.

It was down to him to say something.

She was nothing if not traditional.

Thankfully, he caught her hint.

With a stretch and a slight yawn, Monty drew the towel which had been lying beneath him on the sun lounger about his shoulders and looked her in the eye. "Hey," he said, "You wouldn't want to go for a drink in the bar later, would you?"

Joan grinned back at him. "I'd love to."

2

JOAN RINSED HERSELF OFF with an icy cold shower and then she perused the options available to her in the wardrobe. She'd brought a whole host of dresses out here with her, anticipating that she'd have a whole host of functions to go to in the evenings. What she hadn't banked on was just how the sun seemed to drain her. Until tonight, she hadn't been able to do much else save collapse down into her bed and sleep away till the morning.

She took special care to brush her teeth, to get herself shot of all the bits of lemon from the lemonade she'd been drinking earlier, and then she puffed on a little of the peach-scented perfume she'd brought along with her.

It wasn't anything expensive, but she liked the way it smelled.

She stood in front of the mirror, staring back at herself in the dress.

It was a light-blue number—simple, and it came down to just below her thigh. One of those summer dresses that, back in England, she might get the chance to wear—to *really* wear— perhaps only two or three times a year.

She loved the feel of the silky material against her skin, the way that it seemed to stroke her. With all her preparations done for— what might well turn out to be—a Night of Love, she shucked on out through the door and off towards the hotel bar.

The bar itself was located in a large, glass room which, Joan was sure, would be nigh unbearable during the day with the sun shining at full strength. Now, though, with all the windows thrown wide and with the sound of the sea lapping the shore coming through, it was something approaching paradise.

The whole place was lit up by candles, and the small, round

tables were all covered in white table cloths. Already there were a few other guests scattered about the room: overweight middle-aged men and their wives—kids all in bed—staring out inanely through the window to the sea, their drinks sitting on the table before them, half-forgotten for the time being.

There was no music—neither live or coming through the speakers—and Joan was glad, because this whole scene was so peaceful. It was all such a perfect way to spend the summer.

Monty soon arrived to the bar. Tonight he wore a white shirt over a pair of loose, beige trousers. He kept the shirt untucked and unbuttoned so as to show off the cleavage of his pectoral muscles.

Joan noticed the middle-aged man—but especially the middle-aged man's wife—having a good look at Monty as he approached.

"Evening," Monty said with a smile, and then bent down into her and planted a soft kiss on Joan's cheek.

Joan couldn't help but blush—long and hard—as if she had been transported back to the fifties where a kiss on the cheek—*in public no less!*—fell nothing short of a scandal.

Monty took up the seat opposite her.

When the waiter came by to take their order, Monty insisted on ordering for the both of them. He went for a pair of dry martinis.

Joan could feel herself squirming just a touch on her bar stool. There was something—something about tonight—that she just couldn't quite get her head around. This whole trip out here, to this 'summer job', it had all been somewhat unreal . . . and this moment wasn't much different.

"So," Monty said, "What made you come out here for no pay?"

Joan felt her chest tighten just a little. She looked back into his dark blue eyes and said, "Michael paid for my flights out here—all the airport transfers too—I get the free room, all the food I could eat. Everything here is free. I guess if I'd taken a summer job I'd maybe be able to bank a little, but, for the most part, I'd just be working to pay the bills on my room."

"You not paying your room now, then?"

Joan shook her head. "Nah, I let it go. I'll find another place when I go back to university in the autumn. But until then I can enjoy this nice, free time."

There was a period of silence as the waiter set their drinks down before both of them.

Joan stared into her drink—into the clear liquid—and she wondered whether she had really imagined things would be as perfect as they were here . . . and right now.

Monty lifted his glass, held it up to hers, and they clinked them together.

When they'd drunk, Monty continued, "Not got a family home you can stay at during the holidays, then?"

Joan felt her gut clench. Why did everybody always want to talk about their families? Family, at least for her, was greatly over-rated. She had left home at sixteen and not looked back. "Nah," she said, setting her glass back down.

"I mean," Monty continued, "you could have got a job and stayed at home—that way you could've saved more money."

Joan forced a smile, but she wished—more than anything—that the conversation would turn off in some other direction. "Didn't fancy it," she finally said. "This way I cut my expenses to nothing for the summer, and that's worth it."

For a while, they just sat there, their drinks in hand, and stared out at the lapping waves on the beach. Joan liked it better when they didn't speak. That was the best part of all of this—the *not* speaking. She didn't need to know anything about Monty, and Monty didn't need to know anything about her.

Did she need to come out and say it so plainly?

When they'd finished their drinks—Monty was a gentleman

and he took his drink down at the same pace she drank hers—
Monty paid for the two of them, despite Joan's protests to go
Dutch. Monty looked across the table, deep into her eyes in a way
that made her squirm and he said, "Want to take a walk on
the beach?"

3

T HE SAND WAS FINE and smooth between Joan's toes. It still felt a little warm from the sunlight that'd beamed down on it all day. She walked beside Monty, who was also barefoot. A very slight breeze blew over the ocean and caught her hair in its grasp. Every couple of steps, Joan had to untangle her hair from her eyes, but she enjoyed the sensation.

Joan could still taste the slightly bitter lemony gin on her tongue, and it seemed to somehow work flawlessly with the sweet smell of the ocean air. The sea continued to lap into the shore, and she toyed with it, seeing how close she could get to the water without dipping so much as a toe into it.

Joan enjoyed the near silence as they walked along the shore. She could hear her heart beating hard in her eardrums, and the gentle *thump-thump* of her blood at her temples—the way that she always felt after a day spent out in the glare of the sun.

When Joan looked to Monty, she saw him looking out over the waves, out to the horizon, and she couldn't help wondering about that luscious body she'd seen a little earlier on the sun lounger. It was then that she found herself saying, "How long are you going to stay?"

"Hmm?" Monty said, not turning away from the ocean.

He seemed preoccupied with something.

For a cynical moment, Joan wondered if he was just putting on that lame profound act all the pretentious boys liked to try from time to time. That look which showed them to be a deep thinker. Which *hinted* that they had depths to them . . . when most of the time, Joan was sure, they were simply mentally undressing her.

Or some other girl.

Monty turned back to her slowly. He gave her a gentle smile. He closed the gap between the two of them with a pair of steps, and then he said, the smell of gin still strong on his breath, "Does it really matter?"

Joan stared up at him, into his dark blue eyes, and the yellow-white glow of the moon reflected in them, and she could, already, feel herself being swept away. Resistance was futile now. She could simply do nothing more.

And, with a gentle gesture, she shook her head.

4

THE NEXT MORNING, Joan could feel her whole body tingling all over. She lay in bed with the first rays of the sun shining on in through the netted curtains of her bedroom. She felt damp with sweat, as she always did with the humid nights here. She only realised how widely she was smiling when she glanced up to the mirror which faced the bed.

She breathed in, took in that scent of Monty's cologne, and the smell of his sweat.

She took it in deeper still.

And then breathed it out.

Looking out through the netted curtains, out into the car park her room looked out on, she knew that she would need to get showered and dressed soon, that she would need to park her buns on the sun lounger before too long.

Another day at the office, she thought with a wry smile.

She turned over onto her side.

There was nobody there.

Only the obvious signs that the sheets had been disturbed: the slight indentation on the pillow beside her own where Monty had laid his head afterwards and stared into her eyes.

She really hadn't known what she'd expected.

Did she think that he was going to stay here for the rest of the night?

Was that it?

Had she expected him to make her feel like a lady and not some cheap call girl?

Did she really feel badly about it herself?

She turned her thoughts back to the night before. She thought about how they'd gone for that drink at the bar, and then that walk on the beach, and then—*finally*—they'd come back here.

To her place.

There hadn't been any illusions.

This was a holiday romance, and Joan knew that.

And so did Monty.

Still smiling, Joan slipped out from beneath her sheets and headed off to go get a shower.

When she emerged, she opened up her hotel room door to find that there was a fresh bikini awaiting her there, already on its hanger.

Today it was a red one—*Somewhat appropriate,* she thought with a minxy grin, *Given the night of unbridled passion.*

When she arrived at her sun lounger, she found that Monty was already there, that he was lying back, those cheeky Speedos of his tightened about his waist. He craned his neck back at her and gave her a smile.

She smiled at him too.

After Joan'd got herself settled in, the morning sun still on the rise, and the waiter bringing out her daily ration of a glass of lemonade, she noticed the gentle buzz of the morning people, all of them walking along the shore.

She caught the glances off the men—both attached, and otherwise—and she watched their glances skip past her, slip upwards, to the hotel behind. And she wondered how many of them would get in touch with their agents, decide to switch to the Mediterranean Arms. But that, as Joan reminded herself, was somewhat past her remit.

When she glanced back over at Monty, she saw that he was staring back out to sea, that his mind was already on other things.

She drew in a deep breath, tasting the sea breeze, and she thought to herself about how, even if this *was* a holiday fling—and she wasn't under any pretence that it *wasn't*—then at least it would be a lengthy one.

She still had seven weeks to go, after all.

Seven weeks in paradise.
And all expenses paid.

LOVE SHOULD NEVER WAIT

1

EVEN THOUGH Lisa had stopped on the way to the school to get changed out of her boring, charcoal-toned work skirt and her dull-as-all-hell white blouse; she didn't hold out much hope for *Lovers Leap!*

But, still, it seemed more promising than *Basket Makers Anonymous*.

At least for her purposes, which was to say, *illicit* man-hunting purposes.

Still, speed dating, it did seem like another level of desperate . . .

For tonight, she'd gone with a cool, turquoise summer dress, in order to really bring out her green eyes which—judging from the way her slew of dates went on about them above all else—were her A-Grade feature.

Pity that outside it felt like it was going to snow later.

And in *April*.

Still, at least the inside of the school seemed to have some sort of central-heating system.

Budget cuts hadn't seen fit to turn the thermostat down a few notches in the evening.

Yet.

Lisa breathed in deeply, taking in the smell of disinfectant, hastily smeared onto the floors of the afterhours school building. She'd come across a cleaner or two on her way to the classroom here. They'd pop up from just about any place:

A seemingly deserted classroom.

An apparently empty hallway.

Even when Lisa had got out of her car, a cleaner had— somehow—found her way just beneath her elbow, looking some-what menacing as she wielded a mop and bucket.

Lisa could still taste the strawberry-flavoured cereal bar she'd

unceremoniously munched on during the drive over here—
returning from the Big Smoke, where she'd, as always, been
extremely pleased to leave her design-gimping at *HelMat Smiles:
Media & Marketing Services.*

Pleased to leave behind her tiny cubicle, everything precari-
ously balanced into a series of piles and nothing ever—*seemingly*—
where she'd left it.

Already, as Lisa stepped into the makeshift *Lovers Leap!*—a
maths classroom in another life, by the look of the work stapled up
on the walls—she could hear the excited *chatter* of the other
attendees.

Her stomach dipped.

Although Lisa had sent her money along—made the direct
deposit online, printed out her confirmation—she, for some
reason, hadn't quite squared with herself the idea that she would
ever actually *arrive* here.

But here she was . . .

As Lisa looked about the blue plastic chairs—all of them,
without exception, smeared with penned-on graffiti—she couldn't
help but think one thought to herself:

A lot of women here tonight . . .

In fact, was there even *one* man among them?

She glanced over the dozen or so beaming faces: all of them
stuck into recently-acquainted chatter.

And all of them, without exception, *women.*

Lisa wondered if she had maybe—*unwittingly*—set herself up
for some kind of a lesbian dating ring. She thought back to the
publicity on the website. Reminded herself of those stock photos
which'd featured couples—*heterosexual* couples.

No, she was quite certain that *Lovers Leap!* was just what she
was in the market for.

She smiled vaguely at the already-assembled women,
reminding herself, as she took her seat in one of the lesser-graffi-

tied chairs near the front of the classroom, that these women were her competition.

Most of them, from what she could tell from the reflection in the window of the classroom, were touching, or a little over, forty.

And Lisa, having just notched up *thirty*, believed herself to have the early advantage.

In her mind, at work today, she had been daydreaming about meeting a single-father—*divorced, living alone*—no attachments, no childcare duties past weekend visits and an evening here or there.

No *pressure* on her.

And plenty of spare time.

That was the thing about the City Men, they were just too busy. They were constantly on the move. Having a meeting here; going to their gyms or sports clubs there. Going out with friends and, no doubt, ending up in all sorts of sordid locales in the early hours.

Not that Lisa would *ever* find out the truth.

Oh, no, that would be in direct contravention to the 'Bros' Code'.

... Dickheads, all of them ...

Lisa tentatively laid her handbag down on the equally graffitied table top. She snapped open the catch and pawed about inside. She located the bare essentials: compact mirror, mascara and lipstick. She removed all three and went to work, touching up what she might've missed as she'd done her makeup while sitting in traffic on the way here.

That done, and slipping a surreptitious breath mint in for good measure, Lisa felt that she was feeling good and ready for the *romantic* night ahead.

Or *whatever* sort of a night tonight turned out to be ...

Because, with a quick glance about the classroom again, she realised that there was—*still*—not a single man in the room ... no pun intended ...

The sturdy, steel-framed clock which hung up above the whiteboard ticked away to itself, moving the long minute hand along another notch.

Lisa did *feel* like she was back in school.

She sucked the breath mint into nonexistence.

Breathed out her now-fierily minty breath and then leaned back a little in her chair.

And felt the wood give a little.

She tried not to let it worry her.

The smart *clack* of heels sounded in the hallway outside the classroom and, in no time at all, a perfumed, poufed woman in her fifties—wearing a short, black skirt with diamond-patterned tights—strutted into the room.

She clasped a computer tablet and, it seemed to Lisa, she didn't let up that surely computer-designed smile of hers for a matter of minutes before deigning to address the room. As she opened her red-painted lips, her eyes paused in their investigation. She let out a small, almost sad, "*Hmm,*" and then, with a quick peek at her tablet, frowned some more.

As if nobody had been watching, the woman gave a slight shrug and turned on the smile once more. "Ladies, and, well . . . *ladies!* Allow me to welcome you to *Lovers Leap!* May you find all that you desire."

Lisa recognised that last fragment as being the tagline *Lovers Leap!* used on their website.

The woman continued, "My name is Dana and I shall be your matchmaker for the evening."

There was a long pause as 'Dana' tapped away at her tablet, frowned at something else, and then, with a fierce swipe, seemed to locate what she was looking for.

She turned on the smile once more.

"Now, we seem to be missing a few for tonight"—her smile widened—"has *anybody* seen any rogue men floating about the premises?"

It took a couple of seconds before the joke dribbled through to the group's understanding.

Lisa literally curled her toenails in her shoes.

She breathed in the synthetic odour of her lipstick, and longed to feed herself another breath mint. She was at *that* stage of the day when she felt like every breath she breathed was raw sewage.

For a couple of moments, the heating in the classroom seemed to go on the blink. She felt a harsh draught creep up the backs of her bare calves.

Seriously, April, who would've thunk it?

She thought she heard a distant door whisper shut.

All the doors around the school were fitted with those safe-closing mechanisms.

A kind of hydraulic arm, or whatever the hell the technical name for it was . . .

Anticipating that Dana was about to strike up her speech once more, Lisa anticipated her, raising her hand up lean and proud.

It was almost like she was back in school.

Dana didn't notice right away, a sound emanated from her mouth along the lines of, "Bleh . . ." before she broke off and gifted Lisa with her full and undivided attention.

"Yes?" Dana said, a pressing staccato.

"May I be excused?" Lisa asked.

Dana blinked several times, as if considering the question from all angles and then, tilting her head to one side, and closing her eyes ever so slightly, she said, "Of course you may—but remember that we're *out of hours* now."

Lisa felt herself blush a little at this remark, and she heard the collected women at the back of the classroom give a slight titter at the joke—had they been on the wine before coming out here?

Lisa hoiked herself up, handbag and all, and got herself—*thank-fully*—clear of the disaster zone.

2

LISA HAD MADE IT about halfway down the hallway, to the exit which led to the car park, when she smelled—*distinctly*—the odour of cigarette smoke. She stopped dead. Sniffed at the air. Felt those pleasant *smoky* memories returning. Those memories of when she had been at art college.

And she had got through a pack a day.

Just like everyone else, the motivating factor for her to quit had been the Smoking Ban: when it was no longer permissible for Lisa to smoke while she worked at her latest project in the art studio.

She had enjoyed smoking. It'd been a pleasant past time. But she had never been addicted . . . or, at least, she had never been addicted *enough* to want to go and stand outside in frost-filled air, shielding a flimsy flame with a cupped hand.

That was the stuff of junkies.

There was a real thrill to smelling cigarette smoke in a school. Although Lisa had always been far away from being one of the Bad Girls, she had always got something of a kick from smelling cigarette smoke coming from the toilets—knowing that something deeply illicit was going on.

She glanced up the hallway, back to the classroom, where she could hear Dana's voice punching out some sort of sales blurb, or message, or *command*.

Lisa sniffed at the air some more.

She should just get going.

This evening had been a total washout and it wasn't worth dwelling on it.

But *that* smell.

Perhaps just a little diversion . . .

Before she could really get her thoughts together into any semblance of order, Lisa found herself trudging off in the direction of the smoke. When it reached its *strongest*, she glanced up to see that it was the boys' toilets.

Could she go in here?

Weren't there . . . *laws* against her going inside?

Probably.

She took a few steps in through the doorway, and the stench of urine and urinal cakes—not to mention *more* of that disinfectant the cleaners were so keen on using—almost knocked her backward. But the strong smell of the cigarette smoke enticed her in further.

Sent that *buzz* through her blood.

As she turned the corner, as the light-blue tiles receded and she caught sight of the smoker within, she saw that it was a man, maybe around his late forties, early fifties. He wore a smart, black suit—no tie, and his shirt undone a couple of buttons. He had a full head of silver hair and his face was a little leathered, apparently from the sun. He stood with his elbow propped up against the sill of the frosted glass, peering out to the obscured scene beyond. He had left the smaller window, located at the top of the main one, open all the way on its latch, and he was blowing smoke out through it.

Or at least making the effort to aim in its general direction.

Lisa felt her chest tighten. Her heart hammered. And she tasted that ashen, yet familiar, flavour all the way to the back of her throat. It was one of those feelings that almost felt like she was coming home after being years abroad.

Like she was revisiting a long-lost childhood.

She should go.

She should just slip out while . . .

The man turned his head towards her.

His brilliant blue eyes stuck her like a pair of daggers.

He held the cigarette firmly between his fingers. It smouldered away, sending up neat twin spirals of white smoke. He seemed to regard her for several moments. He seemed to have no fear of getting caught smoking here.

He gave her a smile. "Thought I could get away with a quick one," he said, his voice, all at once, quick and gruff, and *no-nonsense*. "No point in going out for a smoke only to catch a chill, now, is there?"

Lisa found herself struck dumb for a good few seconds.

In the distance, she could still hear Dana chirping on about this or that, or the other.

Lisa snapped herself out of her voluntarily-muted state. "Uh," she started, unconvincingly, "I'm . . . *sorry*."

He gave her a stare, took another drag of his cigarette, and then flicked the butt up and out through the tiny, latched-open window with practised skill.

Lisa lost herself in the arc of the cigarette butt's trajectory. She watched it loop neatly through the gap and then out of sight behind the frosted glass. She had to remind herself to look at the man, who was now rapidly approaching her, his hand outstretched.

"Name's Anthony Twochurch," he said.

"Oh," Lisa got out, imagining herself as some kind of distressed maiden in a novel of manners. Then she remembered herself. What she had come here *to do*. She held out her hand. And shook his. He had a firm grasp. A few callouses; roughed-up, working hands . . . just how she liked them.

Finally, she recalled the unwritten rules of polite introduction. Specifically the article about reciprocity. "I'm Lisa," she said, and then added, since there seemed to be a vaguely formal tone to proceedings, "Lisa Dovetop."

" 'Dovetop?' " Anthony said, arching a thick, but well-trimmed, silver-grey eyebrow. "That's an odd name."

"I could say the same about 'Twochurch', " she responded, bluntly.

This raised a smile in him.

She only realised that he was still holding her hand when he let go.

When his warm skin was no longer pressed up against hers.

"Seems almost like it's meant to be," Anthony said.

Lisa allowed *that* statement to hang in the air of the boys' toilets for a few seconds.

When Anthony saw that no reply was forthcoming, he put in, "What's the state-of-play like for tonight?"

Lisa turned her mind back to the classroom.

For some reason, it seemed like it was a remnant of some past life now.

Something that had been deeply *arduous* to escape.

Lisa tried out a smile, hoped there wouldn't be too many give-away kinks in her voice. "Lots of women," Lisa said, and then added, "Actually, there're *only* women."

Anthony arched an eyebrow again—this time the other one. "Well, that's a surprise," he said, not sounding surprised at all. He breathed in deeply and then sighed out again. "There's usually another fellow who comes along, but I guess he's decided to cut his losses. Didn't come last week either—*bunked off.*" He stared deeper into Lisa's eyes. "His loss."

Lisa held herself still. She was afraid that she might tremble out of control if she allowed the situation to get to her. Although she knew it was a cliché, she *did* feel as if she could quite easily cut the tension in the room with a knife.

And not a particularly *sharp* knife.

"Do you, uh," Lisa said, "want to go someplace?"

" 'Someplace?' " Anthony said, and then smiled wider. "Sure."

Lisa managed to lighten up just a little. "You're buying," she said, and then turned and stepped out of the boys' toilets.

3

THEY TOOK THEIR SEPARATE CARS, and, following a brief discussion, Lisa decided to go on Anthony's recommendation and go to a fish restaurant located a little way into town.

A *safe* distance from the school.

The restaurant was packed full, and the windows were steamed up. The smell of garlic butter screwed up through the air, tantalising Lisa's nostrils. Making her whole body tingle with anticipation. The air was filled with *chatter*, but not the same nervous, desperate stuff which'd filled that maths classroom back at the school; *no* this was contented, happy chatter between people who deeply cared about one another.

The waiter gave Anthony something of a knowing smile—Lisa would have to watch her step *there*—and seated them off at a table nestled in the corner of the restaurant.

The table was covered with a pristine, white tablecloth, and there was cutlery which, if it wasn't *actual* silver, was very nicely polished.

A candle burned away in the neck of a long-ago emptied green wine bottle which sat on the table between the two of them.

Once they'd ordered—Lisa went with the mussels, while Anthony went with the crab—Lisa decided to press Anthony for more information.

She immediately garnered—or perhaps Anthony freely surrendered—that he had a young son attending the school where *Lovers Leap!* took place. Other than to say that the boy lived with his mother, Anthony really had nothing else to add.

And Lisa was in no mood to press him.

Wasn't *all* that interested, really.

When their dishes arrived—along with a glass of fizzy water

for the two of them: since they were both driving—Lisa tucked into her mussels tentatively, partly because she didn't want to come across as a pig at a trough to Anthony, but also because she wanted to catch sight of Anthony's table manners.

No elbows.

Napkin tucked into the collar of the shirt.

Sleeves of shirt rolled up neatly.

Well, he seemed pretty much impeccable.

But, mind what she thought, those manners really did have a habit of slipping.

She'd give them maybe three, four months, at the most.

That was the thing about divorced men. There was always *some* reason why they were back on the market: even if it was a case of only one previous female owner.

The trick was to find out as soon as possible.

They were waiting around for desert when Lisa caught her first clue as to what this reason might be. It was as she was dabbing her lips with her napkin that she caught Anthony slipping his mobile out of his pocket, frowning momentarily at the screen, tapping away for a moment or so, before replacing it.

Ah, so it was work . . . the man was a workaholic.

When Anthony glanced up, he didn't apologise for this quick flip through his mobile, or, if he did, he hoped that it was conveyed by his gentle smile.

And those brilliant blue eyes.

Those eyes which made her think of the depths of the Caribbean.

For dessert, Lisa had a chocolate tart while Anthony went for the lemon sorbet.

Even as she'd ordered the chocolate tart, Lisa had regretted it, already showing her inner glutton to the man who—*might well*— turn out to be the One.

Or, at the very least, *one* of the Ones.

With dinner all over and done with, they ordered coffee . . . always a good sign that the 'date' was going well. Lisa decided that she wanted to know a little more about Anthony's involvement with *Lovers Leap!*

She sipped at her cappuccino, her heart now thumping along at a far steadier rate. As she brought the cup back down onto the table, she peered over the table at Anthony and said, "What happens when there's only one man at *Lovers Leap?*"

Anthony smirked a touch. He set his own cappuccino down in its saucer. "Well, let's just say that, as the sole man, you turn into the centre of attention."

"Even with a quick smoke beforehand?"

Anthony shrugged. "Didn't seem to make much of a difference that I observed."

"But, I mean, how this speed-dating thing works, I thought that there needed to be an equal number of men, and women."

"Yes," Anthony said, "you're probably right."

"Then why don't they make sure—*beforehand*—that they'll have equal men and equal women?"

"Don't know," Anthony said, with a shake of his head and a slightly dazed smile. "I've never really put much thought into it, to be honest."

Lisa found herself locked onto Anthony's blue eyes, and she told herself to act a little more coy—*dammit!*—so she slipped her eyes out of focus a touch, melding their surroundings: the diners, the wallpaper, the candlelight; into one big greyish, white blur.

"And what about if there's only women?"

Anthony shrugged. "I suppose that *Lovers Leap!* are finding out just how to run that particular protocol tonight."

And, although she felt somewhat naughty for doing so, Lisa found herself grinning at this observation.

4

FOLLOWING DINNER THAT NIGHT, Lisa exchanged phone numbers with Anthony, and they went their separate ways. But not before Anthony, clearly having noted her depravity earlier on, offered her a cigarette. Together they'd stood in the fish restaurant car park, each of them puffing away into the chilly April air.

Anthony remarked that he made a point of *not* smoking in his car, seeing as he often had to ferry his son about in it, and he didn't want his son to start smelling like an 'abandonment case', as he put it.

Over the course of the next week, when Lisa returned to work, she surprised herself by being all smiley, and *happy*. Why, she'd thought that *HelMat Smiles: Media & Marketing Services* had successfully crushed that out of her by now.

Apparently not totally.

And what was more was that she found herself, quite giddily, blabbering to anybody who would listen about this Tall, Dark, Handsome Stranger in her life.

Everybody smiled back at her.

Seemed *happy* for her.

But none of them seemed to *truly* understand how she felt.

And how could she really describe it for them?

Put it in terms that they might be able to understand?

With more than a few sighs, as Lisa stood at the photocopier, feeling the warmth from the bright lamp within, breathing in the warm scent of plastic and toner, she speculated that—*really*—nobody would *ever* really understand what went on inside her head.

Just what exactly she *wanted*.

A couple of days later, Anthony called her, asking her to go out with him—*with his son*—on a picnic a little way out in the coun-tryside.

Lisa really didn't know what to say.

She was—*just a little*—taken aback by the hurriedness of the thing.

But she tried to put it out of her mind.

Not worth thinking about really.

When she stood outside her boxy little flat in town, she spotted Anthony right away, driving that *respectable* estate car of his. He pulled up at the curb beside her.

Just like she remembered him in her mind, he was constantly smirking, as if there was some private joke constantly in play with him.

And Lisa couldn't help thinking that the joke was at her expense.

The first thing she noticed, when Anthony pulled up, was that there was no sign of his son in the back seat. Or in the front seat.

Although Lisa didn't wish to bring this up, she simply had to cut through the small talk after a few minutes, to ask Anthony directly where his son was.

They were sat at a set of traffic lights and while Anthony replied to her, he became deeply agitated. He dragged his athletic, leathery fingers through his silver hair.

Lisa could tell that he was riled about what'd gone on.

He told her that his son's mother—*his ex-wife*—had told Anthony that he couldn't take out his son to go and meet Lisa. That she had been totally against the idea. All the time that he spoke, Anthony continued to face forwards, staring at the pulled-up car right in front of them. At first Lisa believed that Anthony was just being cautious, that he didn't want to be caught flat-footed when the lights changed. Then Lisa thought it was for another reason.

That he didn't want to make eye contact with her.

And that *did* ring alarm bells.

But Lisa said nothing at all.

Because Anthony seemed really caught off-beat by the whole episode.

Finally, they shifted off into the traffic, with Anthony belting along a good ten miles per hour over the speed limit.

Even if Lisa wouldn't admit it to herself, she was a little frightened.

She gripped the plastic handle tightly as Anthony flew through the streets and out of the town.

5

THE REST OF THE DAY was wonderful.

And Lisa soon forgot the morning experience.

Anthony picked them out a fresh little glade, a lake off in the near distance, its grey-blue water gleaming at them in the warm sun which blazed down. They sat with the wicker picnic hamper beneath an old, knobbled oak tree.

There was *something* about oak trees that always made Lisa feel comfortable. Now, she was a long way off being the proverbial 'tree-hugging' hippy, but even she had to admit that there was a special power in knowing that these enormous feats of nature stood scattered throughout the world.

These feats which were *so much* greater than she was.

Lisa leaned herself up against the thick, rough bark of the tree, and breathed in its *earthy* scent. In the near distance, she could hear the *buzz* of insects, and the light *gush* of the breeze as it passed over the long blades of grass.

For their picnic lunch, Anthony had packed smoked-mackerel pâté, along with some freshly-baked baguette he had apparently bought from a bakery before picking her up.

They sat, more or less in silence, each of them chewing on their respective lunches.

Although Lisa knew that she couldn't say so much out loud, she was glad Anthony hadn't brought his son along for this day out. It would've utterly changed the day.

Beyond recognition.

She just enjoyed the thick flavour of the smoked mackerel smothered onto her baguette, more or less in silence. She breathed it in, and, with the grass surrounding her, she couldn't quite believe how close she felt to the world in that exact moment.

Anthony produced a bottle of white wine a little while after lunch.

Just a small bottle.

Enough for two glasses.

Maybe three.

Anthony served himself a very small amount while he brought Lisa's own glass brimming almost to the surface. When Lisa brought her glass of wine to her lips, she felt the chilly liquid spill down her chin, the smell of the alcohol a little sharp to her nostrils.

But intoxicating *too*.

And, before long, she could feel herself falling drunk.

Utterly and unsalvageably.

When she surfaced to the world around her, glanced back along the glade, she realised that Anthony was staring at her with a fixed expression. And though she couldn't identify what drew her attention to him so completely right then, she decided, later, that nobody—*ever*—had looked at her in that way before. The way that it seemed, even if an aeroplane came dive bombing out of the clouds, crashed right down into that lake a little way off, in clouds of greyish-black smoke and the screaming of engines; he wouldn't even break off his look at her.

So, when Anthony leaned in her, his mouth open—*hungry*—and his hands fumbling at the back of the summer dress she wore that day, she couldn't do much else but give herself to him.

At least there had seemed no other option *then*.

6

L ISA BEGAN TO FEEL STRANGE about her and Anthony's developing relationship more or less directly after that experience—the *picnic*. First of all, Anthony didn't call her for several days.

Lisa soon identified this as, maybe, having something to do with what she had spotted in him on that very first day. How, when they'd sat in that fish restaurant, Anthony had been tapping away at the screen of his mobile, apparently attending to some Very Important Business Indeed.

She supposed that he had lost himself down the rabbit hole of his *job* . . . just like men of that age are wont to do.

But Lisa told herself to be patient.

She clammed herself up at work, put off that whole giddy act she'd been almost unwary of. She went back to being, pretty much, a design gimp. Completing whatever it was that the company demanded of her. Pimping her brain for an hourly rate.

It wasn't until the weekend—not until a Saturday evening— that Anthony called her up again.

When Lisa answered the phone, she was already in her pyjamas.

She had just got out of the bath, could still feel that warm sensation all over her skin, that slightly tingly feeling of all her pores being open. When she caught sight of who it was calling, she thought about just leaving it all. She wasn't much in the habit of playing games with men.

But there was something *about* Anthony which drew her in.

Whenever she thought that she had got Anthony loose from her mind, he would come crawling back into her consciousness. Never really gone at all.

But that wasn't enough to make her pick up the phone.

As she did hold her phone to her ear, she could already conjure —in her mind—his musky scent in her nostrils. She could *feel* his taut muscles pressed up against her.

His insistent mouth.

And she had to see him again.

Although she didn't necessarily want it that way, Lisa had had no time to clean her place this weekend. She never seemed to have time to do anything these days. Work seemed to take over just about everything that wasn't covered by thoughts of Anthony, and, when not at work, she seemed to find other things to do: brew some coffee, make some toast, flip on the TV; lose a few hours that way.

Anthony turned up at her flat within the hour. He was smirking slightly, like always, and dressed in a prim, well-cut suit. As he stood on her doorstep, she remarked at how he seemed *larger*. How she hadn't really appreciated just *how big* he really was.

They watched a film for maybe half an hour before they were in one another's arms.

Until they proceeded to the bedroom.

7

AFTER *THAT* OCCASION, however, Lisa didn't hear from Anthony for a full two weeks. And she actually went to the trouble of calling *him*. But she got no answer. He was all tied up, Lisa supposed, with that theoretically Very Important Job of his.

She tried not to let it get to her . . . and yet, at the same time, Lisa couldn't shake the feeling that she felt somewhat cheated by this whole affair. Hadn't the reason she'd gone to *Lovers Leap!* been to bag herself a man just like Anthony?

Hadn't the idea been to have a man who *had* time to spend on her?

To have a man who wasn't still *obsessed* with his work?

Was that too much to ask?

When a month had passed without any call from Anthony, Lisa decided that she was just better off drawing a line under the entire episode. Why should she wait for someone like Anthony when, most likely, there was a whole line of fifty-something men forming a queue to take a thirty-something like her out.

So it was with that intention Lisa decided to give *Lovers Leap!* a try.

Only when she pulled up in the school car park did she recall how it had been before. An entire *roomful* of women all sat there, in that maths classroom. If she *was* looking for a man then *Lovers Leap!* surely should be quite a way down a *long* list of possible locales to strike up a hunt.

Lisa sat in her car, the vibrations of the engine throbbing through her palms as she gripped the steering wheel tightly. She stared through the windscreen, out at the exterior, cement wall of the school. She could see that it had been white washed, probably, hundreds of times. Graffiti still showed through many of the layers.

She should just go.

There was *nothing* up there in that maths classroom.

Just women ten years her senior.

No *men.*

But Lisa had come all this way.

It would be a waste of time if she *didn't* go.

And she'd already made the direct deposit that afternoon.

Lisa helped herself out of her car, allowing her seatbelt to fling off her shoulder and slingshot back into its holder, the sable belt kept snug and out of sight.

As Lisa trod her way along the hallway, directed for the maths classroom, she could hear the excited voices, all of them crowing about within.

Those *women*, all over again.

But there was something different this time—something which drew her attention.

They were all laughing, and joking.

It almost—*almost*—seemed as if they were laughing and joking about Lisa.

But she tried to put that thought out of her mind.

As Lisa turned into the doorway, she took in all the women sat within. All of them perched on the far too-small wooden seats. She glanced to Dana, who stood up before them all, clutching a computer tablet.

When Lisa turned her head to the room, she was surprised to see a whole group of men—*surely as many as there were women*—huddled on the other side of the classroom. The only difference with the men was that they weren't speaking at all to one another. They all remained steeped in silence, diligently staring towards the front.

Lisa slipped Dana an apologetic smile, and took up her place at one of the seats. Cramming herself in again behind one of those well-graffitied desks, plumping her handbag down on the surface.

As Dana spoke to them, going through some spiel, or other, Lisa heard somebody making a "*Psst!*" sound almost right in her ear.

When Lisa eventually craned her neck back, took in the speaker, she saw that it was one of the women. Though, who else would it have been? The woman wore a violet blouse with a frumpy front to it. One of those ragged, birdlike constructions which, Lisa had to admit, she had never been much a fan of.

The woman was well made up, too.

She had on dark eye shadow and her skin seemed almost plastered with concealer.

Several shades too tanned for her skin tone.

"He did it, didn't he?" the woman said, her voice low, conspiratorial.

Though Lisa was fairly certain to which 'he' the woman referred, she didn't want to jump the gun just yet. This seemed like one of those open questions which just begged for her to give the obvious answer . . . and thus be well and truly *laughed* at.

And, if Lisa couldn't stand one thing, it was being laughed at.

Then again, she supposed that *nobody* really enjoyed being laughed at.

"I . . . uh," Lisa said, casting her glance to the other women sat behind, and to their—equally smiling—faces.

"Not returned your calls, has he?"

"Girls?" Dana's voice came from the front of the classroom. "Is there a problem?"

Lisa felt that *snap* to Dana's voice, and the way it sent a shudder to the bottom of her stomach, as if Dana was a school teacher with some sort of power to *punish* Lisa for having been a naughty girl.

The women shrank back, all giggly and tittering.

Lisa pressed herself harder into her wooden seat. She felt how the flat surface numbed her nerves. She cast a quick glance across the aisle of the classroom, to the men all sitting there in their private, orderly and *extremely* quiet row. She caught a couple of them sending her glances, and she gave them vague smiles in return.

As Dana continued on with her spiel, Lisa heard that woman in her ear once more.

The woman's voice now a strained whisper.

"You should've been a little more patient, the men—the *real* men—they always get here a little late, as if they're *reluctant* to come along."

Lisa continued to face the front. She felt almost like she was a spy, sitting in a public place, pretending that she couldn't overhear the person speaking behind her.

Couldn't hear the message being relayed.

The woman continued, "Did he try on the smoking-in-the-toilets routine with you?"

There was a sustained tingling feeling, down in Lisa's gut.

"It worked, didn't it?"

"Girls?" Dana's voice came, again, from the front. "Is something the matter?"

The woman didn't speak again until Dana crouched down to get something out of the bag she kept at the front. As Dana fished about, the woman spoke again in Lisa's ear. "Don't be upset about it," the woman said, "he's tried it on with all of us—*at one time or another*—difficult to resist . . . I hope you'll forgive us for not speaking up right from the start, from giving you fair warning, but, then again, you never really gave us a chance, did you?"

Lisa felt her mind pitch and turn. She couldn't focus any longer. The world—*the maths classroom*—all those displays on pyramids and prime numbers and, who knew what else, it all distilled in a swirl of black and white.

And then, with a single, distinct *snap*, everything seemed to drift back into place.

She heard the woman's voice for a final time.

"Don't worry about it, love."

Lisa felt the woman's sure hand on her shoulder.

"You'll find someone nice here."

Lisa observed as Dana barked out yet more instructions.

The *squeal* of rubber against the wooden floor, as the tables and chairs were moved about to Dana's whim, was almost deafening for several moments.

As Lisa got herself up to her feet—again at Dana's command—she heard the woman utter something else to her.

"One thing's for certain, though, love should never wait"—a long, distinct pause—"and it should never—*ever*—suffer fools."

PEDESTAL

G RAHAM SLOTTED the freshly plucked rose into the lapel of his jacket and made his way down the red-carpeted stairway where his guests had already accumulated—awaiting his speech for the annual Alcoholism-Recovery-Through-Art spring ball.

The programme he hosted here, in his country home.

In the crowd, he picked out little Ginger. She was his favourite of his friends' daughters. He was glad that she was there. Twenty years old. A little plump. Those hamster-like cheeks.

Perhaps he'd make a pass, when he was a bit drunker and had an excuse.

He produced a spoon from his jacket pocket and rattled it against the side of his champagne glass. After about ten seconds of rattling, the crowd fell into a hush and looked in his direction.

With his face flushed from the alcohol—definitely not from nerves—he grinned at his audience. "My friends! Thank you for being here with me tonight. It's really wonderful to see so many faces, old and new." He cleared his throat. "We're all here tonight to celebrate our successes. Our efforts."

Graham paused, but didn't turn to observe the curtains he knew were dropping behind him. All pre-arranged. From his audience's gasps, he knew the covers had fallen and the painting was revealed.

He continued, reading from the index card placed on the lectern, "It fills me with great pleasure to present Faith Helmsman's piece, 'Infinite Pain'."

Again, he didn't need to turn. He'd seen the picture earlier and hadn't cared much for it. It showed a demon above a fiery pit, standing on a loose rock with angels flying round—in some sort of redemptory fashion.

Who they were trying to redeem was anyone's guess.

"Faith came to us around eighteen months ago," Graham continued, "when she'd reached her lowest point. Her children were taken away from her, she was drinking a bottle of vodka a day and her life was falling down round her ears. However, thanks to David Atkin's help, she's a new person. She has her kids back and life is good again."

Graham indicated David Atkins with his hand.

David stood to one side of the painting looking rather pleased with himself.

After Graham had counted to five in his head, and allowed the polite applause to take its toll, he raised his hand for silence from his public. "Thank you to everyone who supported her."

Graham took a deep breath.

"The next artist has been lucky enough to collect acclaim from the magazine *New Borders*."

Once more, he paused for the attendants to remove the covering from the painting behind him.

This one he *did* quite like, it had a horseman spearing a jaguar —the kind of colonial sentiment he found easy to relate to.

"Daniel Hertford came to us from the street, where he admitted to buying can upon can of Special Brew then blasting his way through them on park benches. One day, he turned up at the gates of the Hall and asked for a second chance." Graham pointed out at the audience. "You gave him that second chance."

There was a huge round of applause, followed by *whoops* as the, still slightly straggly-looking, Daniel stood up next to his piece of work.

Graham clapped along then took a swig of champagne, as the audience wrapped up their self-congratulation.

They knew he was saving the best for last.

His last ex-alcoholic couldn't be kept under wraps.

At the back of the hall, he'd met with men from the national press. They stood out a mile in their unpressed trousers. Indeed, he saw them now—making their way back from the open bar, jostling through the crowd with their large cameras clutched to their chests.

Graham leaned down to the microphone and spoke the words loud and clear, "Frank Small."

The audience flew into a series of *whoops* and *cheers*, as the painting was revealed.

The sound reverberated around the hall and made Graham's ears ring.

He turned to look at the painting: a collection of odd colours and shapes that young people found so appealing. One thing struck him, however, Frank wasn't there.

He'd missed his cue.

Graham turned back to the audience, taking a glance at his cards. He was going to have to adlib—at this point in the show Frank should've been giving his speech.

Graham *hated* adlibbing.

"Um," Graham said into the microphone, then, "Frank?"

There was motion coming from the back of the hall.

Graham hoped it was Frank, but instead a woman channelled through the sea of penguin-suited men. He couldn't help but notice her quite *enormous* bosom which threatened to burst out of the top of her cocktail dress.

Soon, she reached the front of the stage and took the final step in a single leap. She pushed Graham out of the way and seized the microphone.

"Frank is a bastard!"

Graham's eyes opened up wide. What was she doing?

Murmurs among the crowd, uncomfortable with the colloquial language that had slipped into an otherwise formal evening.

"That's right!" she said. "He left me at the bus stop."

More unrest, followed by nudges among the crowd.

"Rubbish!" a voice cried out from within the crowd.

A gunshot rang out in the hall and the next thing Graham knew he was covered in paint.

He looked at the girl, who was covered in green paint—head to toe.

Instinctively, he looked in the direction of the shooter and, sure enough, there was Frank—making his way to the stage with an air rifle in one hand, pointing to the roof.

Once the audience realised, they broke out in wild applause.

Graham glanced at the girl standing beside him and noticed one of her breasts had deflated and hung from her chest.

Apparently the source of the paint . . .

Frank jumped up onto the stage and winked at Graham. He grabbed the microphone. "A round of applause for my accomplice Yvette Berbidge, formally—and soon to be—Yan Thompson."

The audience went crazy.

Women threw off their dainty scarves and men their bowties.

Frank sidled up to Graham and whispered in his ear, "Lights and flashes, eh?"

Graham just smiled back at him.

Though he didn't quite understand, he felt happy having been the one to put Frank on his pedestal.

FATHER'S WATCHING

KERRI JOHNSON sat in the hospital waiting room lightly jigging her leg impatiently. She was going to be late for the interview, and she knew it would be fatal for her chances.

And she badly needed the job too.

Once you got over seventy and you were looking for work, hardly anyone took a second look at you once you stepped through the door for an interview. It was enough for them just to see those wrinkles—she always chuckled to herself when people referred to them as 'battle scars' or 'medals of honour'.

But it was becoming less and less a laughing matter.

She knew that to most of the world she just looked old and useless.

There was no heating in the waiting room so Kerri still wore her woollen plaid scarf, the one she'd got for Christmas from some long-dead uncle well over half a century ago now. She shivered a little and tightened the scarf around her neck, feeling the rough fray of the material, a little scratchy against her skin. She breathed it in too, taking in that musky scent that never seemed to go away even after putting a double dose of detergent in the washer.

Thinking back to that Christmas time, a long time ago, she recalled the carols, the singing, the gentle *crunch* as she stepped through the snow, the first taste of a smoking hot chocolate.

It seemed like another age now.

She eyed the vending machine across from her, listened to its faint buzz, and scrutinised its contents.

All garish colours and fonts she could hardly read without her glasses. She hadn't had time to remember her glasses when she'd got the call to get down here as quickly as possible.

Down the hall she heard faint footsteps and she turned to look.

A doctor, dressed in a crisp, white lab coat, approached her. He had silver hair and his skin was a little tanned, and she wondered whether he'd just got back from a skiing holiday, or perhaps from some sunny beach. But his expression was dour, his eyes sunken in their sockets, and his tan seemed greyer as he drew closer to her.

He shot her with a professional smile, then held out his hand for her to shake. Kerri accepted it. It was funny how manners seemed only to have survived in the medical profession, everywhere else they seemed almost totally lacking. "Mrs Johnson," he said.

"*Ms*," she corrected him.

The doctor gave her a hardier version of his professional smile, beyond which Kerri was sure that she could see the thought, the thought that he really couldn't give a damn flashed bright in his mind. "My name's Doctor Kilner," he said.

That slightly Germanic sounding name sent thrills through her. Ever since she was a little girl her father had always berated them for showing any form of affection for anything that might be German.

Or even mentioning the matter of the War at all.

Her father had served in the War, been a commended soldier. She still had his medals below her bed, nestled in a fireproof protective case. These days, though, she wondered whether she might be able to sell them for something. Her father was long dead, but she still needed heating, needed warmth and food to survive.

Maybe if she missed this job interview she'd have no choice.

Doctor Kilner smiled with the corner of his mouth and talked out of the other. There was nothing about his voice that suggested he was anything other than English born and bred. But, still, she couldn't shake that well-ingrained association. "Your granddaughter is in a coma," he said.

Kerri felt her heart skip a few beats, and that steady coolness inside her turn into an outright chill. She crushed her fingers into fists, and felt her fingernails cutting into her palms.

"Now," Doctor Kilner said, bringing up a clipboard that he'd previously been holding down at his side. He grasped hold of a pencil and glanced over a checklist. "I'd like to ask you some questions about her, if that's all right?"

Kerri felt numbness creeping over her skin. That job interview was a long way off now, as if cut adrift from the forefront of her mind, and disappearing off into the distance on a strong current. She found her mind ravaged with images, with thoughts and feelings, pictures of her granddaughter, how she'd been when she'd been six, seven, eight . . . and then, now, at nineteen years old.

It was heady to even try and get a grip on how much she had changed in all that time.

". . . Ms Johnson? . . . Ms Johnson?"

She looked back at Doctor Kilner, seeing that his professional smile was now replaced by a business-like frown, and she wondered whether he was assessing her, thinking about if he should offer her a check-up with a nurse, 'just to make sure everything's all right' and next thing she'd know she'd be sitting in a nursing home, drooling at the mouth with all the drugs they'd stuck into her.

No, she couldn't do that.

She couldn't *afford* that.

If she wanted a future for her granddaughter, and for herself, then she needed to keep working, to keep putting bread on the table. She was determined that her granddaughter wouldn't end up like her, that she would go to university, get a good job.

That she wouldn't have to graft for no reason at all.

Doctor Kilner looked over his clipboard at her. "I can't tell you what's going to happen next, Ms Johnson, I'm sorry. And I would suggest that you think about going home, about maybe getting some rest. We'll call you if there's any improvement to Nathalie's health."

She glanced up at him, telling herself quite plainly that she wasn't allowed to cry. She hadn't cried in front of a stranger, well . . . since ever. And she had no intention of doing so now. She had to put on that stiff upper-lip that had marked so much of her childhood, from her father's steady berating.

Before she'd consciously made the decision, she found herself getting up, getting to her feet. She gave the doctor one of her stiff smiles and then bundled away, headed for the exit.

The sliding doors swept open for her to reveal the night outside, the snow coming down thick and strong now, layering itself upon the ground.

She paced through the parked cars, their windscreens already iced up, and felt a chilly breeze blow in across her cheeks. She brought her woollen scarf up to cover her mouth and nostrils, then felt her moist breath coming back at her, gently bringing warmth back into her face.

One thing she'd noticed about getting older was how she seemed to get cold all the time.

It had never been like that when she'd been younger, or at least she never remembered it that way.

She guessed she'd spent most of her life rushing about never really thinking anything through, just going onto the next thing, being on her feet constantly had meant her blood had never had a chance to cool.

But it was growing cool now.

And then a thought occurred to her. She pulled back her sleeve and examined her watch. It had a gold-plated wrist strap and the face had Roman numerals that she could remember asking her father how to read when she'd been a little girl, and then she remembered it again, when she'd found it among the things he'd passed onto her when he'd died.

That was all he'd passed on.

That and his medals, and a few debts around town, some tabs to settle in local pubs which she made a point of tracking down. *She* had never been in debt in her life and she was determined never to be in debt with anyone.

That all might change, though, if she couldn't find something, *anything*.

Because she had to provide for Nathalie, give her a proper shot at life. She was certain that Nathalie would do better than she had.

But first things first, Nathalie had to pull out of that coma of hers, and Kerri needed to somehow track down a job.

And from Kerri's first-hand experience with comas she knew that sometimes people just didn't wake up.

She read off the time on the watch. She was about half an hour away from the scheduled time for her interview. She felt her brain pounding, and her heart throbbing in her chest, trying to get fresh, warm blood into her system, trying to stop her shuddering.

Four o'clock in the afternoon and already night.

She tasted that icy coolness in the air, smelled that strange odourless quality of the winter night, and she knew that she had to give it a go. If only for Nathalie.

She had to keep going for her.

Kerri caught a bus going out of town. The fare was one pound eighty, but the driver let her on for one pound. She claimed she had no change, but the truth was that the solitary pound coin was all she had.

The bus ride took about fifteen minutes, and she asked the driver several times, growing more nervous with each repeated asking, for the stop she required.

The driver, apparently brimming with Christmas cheer,

shrugged her off each time, with his monotonous 'No' and she would retake her seat about a metre away from his cabin.

One of the seats assigned specifically for old people and pregnant women.

Her thoughts reeled with Nathalie, thinking of her, how she was getting on. But she had learnt in all her years of living that there were certain circumstances where she was just completely powerless, that simply there was nothing at all she could do.

This was one of those times.

She didn't even need to ring the Stop buzzer when her stop did come up. It seemed to her that the driver had got a handle on exactly where she was headed and was determined that he would get shot of her once and for all.

She thanked him and stepped out through the doors, back into the night, and out along the frosted pavement where she caught a glance at the white fluorescent sign with the blue lettering. A lawyer's firm named *Tuckson and sons*. She hunched her shoulders, allowed herself a single sigh, to get it out of her system, and then barrelled in through the old-style double-hinged doors and into a pleasantly warm waiting room.

When she checked her watch she saw she was ten minutes early.

That was a stroke of luck.

And so she took up a seat on the sofa, as instructed by the kind, grey-haired secretary, and felt herself growing quite cosy there, even though the material was quite rough, and smelled a little of disinfectant. From what she'd understood of the advertisement for the job, she'd seen that this lawyer took on all sorts of clients, and so she guessed some wino single dad or other had been sitting here, warming this seat, not so long ago.

Precisely one minute past the hour scheduled for her interview, the door at the end of the hall swung open with a bright *squeak* of its hinges, and a gruff, but not unkindly, voice called down the corridor.

Kerri collected herself, gripped her handbag tight to her side, and gave the secretary a parting, pleasant smile. The secretary smiled back. And before Kerri knew it she was standing inside the lawyer's office.

The room was boxy and windowless, unless you counted the window hung with those beige vertical hanging blinds that looked out into the corridor Kerri had just walked along. And the room smelled lightly of warmed-cinnamon. When Kerri looked over to the bookshelf which sat behind the desk she saw a joss stick burning there. The scent tickled her nostrils and dried out the back of her throat. She'd never had the type of sensory apparatus that could deal with smoke of any kind. But she knew that, in this situation, it would be impertinent for her to make any comment on it. This lawyer could potentially change her life, and she had to be on her best behaviour.

The lawyer himself was a bulky man in a suit that had probably fitted about five or six years ago. He was now in his forties, or fifties, that was another thing that Kerri had noticed getting older, that she just tended to lose that ability to tell ages with any certainty.

On the bookshelf, in front of those packed-in tomes, *law* books, she saw a couple of silver, or silver-plated, picture frames, featuring photos: a grinning woman and a blond son, his wife and son presumably, and then, beside it, a sepia photograph with a stern-looking man, dressed in an Army uniform.

Kerri recognised the man's dress immediately as a Second World War infantry uniform, just like the one that her father had worn. The way those sepia photographs got after the years, the way they were faded by the sun, it became almost impossible to make out the features of the subject much longer.

If she squinted just so, it was easy to mistake the man there for her father.

The lawyer sat back in his chair, making it creak as he did so. That cinnamon smell got a little thicker in the air and Kerri felt her throat parched. Now she found herself thinking back to that vending machine in the hospital waiting room and she wondered whether she might've spent her last pound coin on a can of drink back there.

But cold drinks on a winter's afternoon, that was just a recipe for getting a cold.

"Ms Johnson?" he said, with a slight hop in his voice, a little out of place considering his bulk.

"Yes," she said, glad that, for once, someone had actually got her name right, hadn't married her off.

He played with the edge of a stack of papers on his desk, whiffling his index finger along the pages, then, slowly, he met her eye. "And you're here about the legal assistant job?"

"That's right."

"Aren't you . . . well"—his gaze wandered in and out of focus, as if he was trying to *unsee* her—"a little old?"

Kerri thought about the dozens of times that statement had come up in these interviews. It had never been this direct before. The first few times she'd been a little taken aback, offended even, and then she'd just learnt to shrug it off.

In a way she was glad about his directness.

She couldn't care less what the law said, she would take someone who called a spade a spade any day of the week, that was just fine in her book.

She realised she still had her scarf about her neck, and she reached up and loosened it a little, let it hang down over her front, not taking it off completely so she'd lose that reassuring tickling sensation of the wool at the back of her neck.

She needed that sensation for when this *lawyer* inevitably turned her down.

"Well?" the lawyer said, arching an eyebrow.

She shrugged. "I need the money."

"Don't you have a pension, something like that?"

"I'm saving."

The lawyer parted his lips slightly. He laid his clutched hands over his chubby gut and then broke off eye contact. Perhaps he would be just like all the others, the ones that couldn't even look her in the eye to tell her that she was just unwanted.

Before he could speak, Kerri sparked up again. "I'm saving up for my granddaughter. I want her to go to university, I never got the chance, you see?"

The lawyer smiled faintly and then that smile disappeared just as quickly. "That sounds wonderful," he said. "Really, wonderful." He glanced back over his shoulder, not turning completely, his massive bulk wouldn't quite allow him. "My family," he said, indicating the photo frame that she'd already looked over.

She nodded and continued to keep up that pleasant smile of hers.

Then the lawyer got all serious. He unclasped his hands, straightened up in his chair, and leant forward. The chair squeaked again and she caught a waft of the man's breath. There was the vague stench of burger grease there—or some other meaty grease —and she felt her throat tighten even more, to the extent that she even considering asking the man for a drink.

It might even earn her a stay of execution.

But, no.

Now it was too late.

Now he was pressing this interview forward to its inevitable conclusion.

"Ms Jackson," he said, the way they always started out, "the problem with this specific role is that it's really, uh, a . . ."

"An entry position?" she said, reading off his patter from experience.

He smiled lightly, as if relieved by her letting him off the hook on this one. She could see that he thought she was going to make it easy on him, wasn't going to cause a scene. "Yes," he said. "It's an *entry* position. And, uh, really it should be filled by someone—"

"Younger?"

He nodded while dialling that pleasant smile of his up a few degrees. Then he drew back to his pleasant, neutral smile, his good will apparently on the cusp of being used up for good. "I'm so glad that we understand one another. You see, the problem is with the advertisement really, I mean, we can't *put* that we need someone young there, that wouldn't be appropriate. But, you see, we can't exactly take anyone on who might be, well, out of the company in a few years' time. Do you understand what I'm saying?"

Now was time for her to bite back a little, to show him that she simply wasn't leaving this office till she'd riled him.

Even just a little bit.

"If that's true then why didn't you tell your secretary to tell me that the post was taken? Wouldn't that have been the easiest way to 'let me down gently' ?"

He parted his lips to respond.

"And don't tell me that you can't tell someone's age from just their voice. You're a *lawyer*. The first thing you'll look for in a secretary is someone who can screen your calls, someone who knows just how to weed people out. And so the question remains. You wouldn't have had me brought in here if you hadn't had the smallest, even the tiniest inkling that you just might take someone like me on."

The lawyer shut his mouth. All the blood seemed to leave his cheeks and his pupils dilated slightly. He reminded her of a young boy she'd scolded once for bouncing a ball up against the wall of the corridor just outside her apartment door. She could still hear that *thunk-thonk . . . thunk-thonk . . .* as the ball had bounced off the floor, hit the wall, then returned to the boy's hand.

That boy hadn't ever returned after his dressing down.

There was a long silence after that. Her words just held up in the air for the longest time. And then the lawyer brought his hand back onto the desk before him. He swirled his finger on the spot, making a sweaty mark with his fingertip.

Kerri decided that now it was time for her to bring out the big guns. If she really could do something about her life—about *Nathalie's* life—then now was the time to do it. She stared at him, willing him to meet her eye. But he kept on staring down at that finger of his. And she just went for it. "My granddaughter is in the hospital. In a coma."

He remained silent.

"Got anything to say to that?"

He kept his gaze firmly fixed down, on his finger still pressed to the table. And then, gradually, he turned his head back up to meet her eye. "I'm sorry to hear that."

"Thank you," she said, and then she nodded to the photograph over the man's shoulder, the one soaked in sepia and showing the uniformed gentleman. "And just who's that?"

The lawyer looked back over his shoulder as if he'd never seen the photo in his life, and then he turned back to Kerri. "My grand-father," he said.

"My father served in the Second World War."

"Is that so?"

His slight tone of indifference wasn't exactly what she'd been looking for, but she supposed that it was a response, and she could always work with a response.

Any response.

She prided herself on it. "And what do you think they'd say now, if they'd been alive? What would they say about this situation? Us here, doing nothing about it."

"About what?"

"Not helping each other out. I remember when I was younger, people would do each other favours all the time. Nothing at stake, just a sense of common purpose. Nowadays, though, that's all gone. Completely puffed up in a cloud of smoke."

He tilted his head toward her, the hint of a smile on his lips now.

"So why not just do something like that? Why not make our descendants proud? Just what they would've wanted."

The lawyer stared at the creases in his palms, and Kerri saw that within those trenches there was a light dousing of sweat glistening there in the sharp light of the office. She knew this man was different from the others, that he had some sense to him, that he could see things from her point of view. But he just needed one further thing, just a little extra, something to push him over the edge.

"Don't think I haven't seen your secretary out there, either, and don't think that I haven't noticed that you gave her a chance. So why not give me one too? I might surprise you."

Then he did meet her eye, and in a thin but steady voice, he said, "You all right to start on Monday?" and then he burst out in a grin and held his hand out across the table.

She shook it, with that firm grip of hers, the one her father had taught her, and then, pride very much intact, she strolled out of his office, back out through the reception. As she stood in the doorway to the lawyer's office, she glanced back at the secretary. She sat there with her horn-rimmed glasses with the strings of plastic pearls holding them hanging round her neck.

And she saw those pale blue eyes of hers, that hint of a smile on her face.

Kerri remembered the practicalities of her situation, then said, "You wouldn't happen to have a couple of quid I could borrow for the bus? I can pay you back on Monday."

The secretary dug into her purse and handed over a handful of change, which Kerri took with a smile. Then she wished the secretary a Merry Christmas before stepping out of the door, into the frosty night air.

The wind blew her silver hair around her face as she waited for the bus. But it had no chance of chilling her now. She felt the warmth glowing out from her chest, and up to her cheeks. It was like her whole ribcage was a furnace. And as she heard the throb of the bus engine approaching, of the snort and slight smell of exhaust as it rounded the corner, she felt her mobile phone vibrating in her handbag.

She pulled it out and answered.

It was Doctor Kilner.

Nathalie was out of the coma.

She was stable.

He was quick to warn her that they weren't out of the woods yet, but it looked good. All being well she would make a full recovery.

Or that was what they hoped.

She replaced the phone in her handbag and stuck out her hand to stop the bus, and it pulled up alongside her with a hiss of hydraulics and a slight screech of brakes. With a final glance back to that lawyer's office, to *Tuckson and sons*, she stepped onto the bus and felt herself whisked away. She remembered being on a sledge as a young girl. That thrill pumping through, that slight dip of her stomach as the sledge whisked down the acute slope. And then getting down to the bottom, and seeing her father there, standing with that broad, winter grin, and the slight pinkness in his cheeks.

Ready and waiting for her.

Keeping an eye on her.

Watching over her forever.

And she couldn't help thinking that he'd been there tonight with her in that office. In the same way she would always be there for Nathalie.

Forever and always.

That was just the way it had to be.

BLANKETY WHITE

1

THE DENTIST'S OFFICE was perhaps Angeline's least favourite place. She hated the slickness of it all, the stiff—and brutally *clean*—furniture. She hated how somebody obviously saw to replacing the magazines on a consistent basis, because, unlike other waiting rooms she frequented, the magazines were never scuffed, or turned at the edges, and they never—*ever*—seemed to lose that glossy shine.

But Angeline really had no choice.

She had toothache.

Well, that was putting it mildly.

It felt like somebody was trying to split her skull open—via her gums—by using a pneumatic drill.

The pain was constant and it seemed never-ending, though it had only got *really* bad this morning.

When the dentist called her into his surgery, Angeline went gladly, and she sat herself down in that cushioned, reclining chair and did her best to relax . . . just like the dentist told her. After she'd finished up with the dentist, he told her that she needed to do some serious flossing, and maybe think about a new brand of toothpaste, which he recommended to her personally.

"What was the name of it?" Angeline said, sitting on the edge of the reclining chair.

That rubbery taste of having had the dentist's gloved hand in her mouth would take an hour or so to shake, she could tell, and the minty smell of disinfectant too. And that was to say nothing for the *whirring* mechanics of the reclining chair. The pain in her mouth wasn't any better either.

"*Blankety White*," the dentist replied, giving her the brand name of the toothpaste.

" '*Blankety*' ?"

The dentist was already busying himself with some paperwork that the dental nurse had handed over to him, and he was flipping through the pages. "Umm, hmm," he finally replied.

Angeline shrugged her shoulders and made a kind of face.

"You can pick up a tube in the reception," the dentist said, not turning away from his folder. "Please keep in mind, Miss . . ."

Angeline noticed the dentist's hesitation and she decided to help him out. "Antherchek."

"Yes, Miss Antherchek, please remember that an *emergency* dental appointment is for just that; *toothache*, I'm afraid, does not qualify."

Angeline caught the dental nurse's eye, and she observed as the dental nurse's grimace turned to a faint smile. No doubt she hadn't expected Angeline to look at her again, the dental nurse had thought that her interaction with Angeline was over and done with.

Not yet.

Not *quite* yet.

Angeline scooped herself up and out of the reclining chair, and she padded across the dental surgery with a pair of faint *goodbyes* from both the dentist and dental nurse.

When Angeline emerged into the reception, she paid up for the appointment, and then glanced to the glass cabinet behind the receptionist. There was a whole assortment of products beneath the glass and, just like every dental office that Angeline had ever visited, none of the products had a price attached to them.

She caught sight of the brand name which the dentist had suggested to her: *Blankety White*, and she pointed it out to the receptionist.

The receptionist produced a small key at the end of a golden chain she kept around her neck. With a neat movement of her delicate wrist, the receptionist popped the glass case open and she removed the tube of *Blankety White*—still nestled inside of its cardboard packaging—and laid it down on the counter before Angeline.

"How much is that?" Angeline said, already digging out her purse.

The receptionist peered down the half-moon glasses which clung to the tip of her nose, and read off some serial number stuck onto the side of the cardboard packaging.

Though Angeline saw the receptionist moving her lips, and making sounds, she wasn't totally sure that she had completely matched up the two. "Come again?" Angeline said.

The receptionist spoke again, and the same thing happened.

The price which tumbled out through the receptionist's lips just couldn't be understood.

Angeline shook her head, blinked a couple of times, and then she glanced back at the tube of *Blankety White* which lay on the counter. "I . . . uh, I think I'll pass, actually."

The receptionist gave the most subtle sigh Angeline had ever heard—so subtle, in fact, that Angeline had to pinch herself to make sure she had *really* heard it. The receptionist padded her way back to the glass cabinet, and she shut the package of *Blankety White* back away. Angeline just paid up and swept on out of the dentist's office.

2

ANGELINE GOT THROUGH most of the day with her mouth pounding like it was on fire, but she did her best to put the sensation out of her mind as she sat at her desk, a phone crooked at her shoulder and her fingers glued to her keyboard, trying to keep up with what the speaker on the other end was telling her.

At five o'clock, when she knocked off for the day, Angeline took a bite into a sausage roll and had to spit it out . . . the toothache had got so extreme that she simply couldn't stomach it any longer. She needed to get her hands on that *Blankety White* stuff.

Although Angeline hadn't bought the *Blankety White* at the dentist's office, and she hadn't regretted *not* parting with the money, she had planned on picking up a tube later on. From some more economical outlet.

In the end, as she clicked and clacked her way on her high heels to the supermarket on the corner of her office, she couldn't help thinking back to the dentist telling her that she was supposed to reserve emergency appointments for *emergencies.*

She probably should've had a go at him for that, who was *he* to judge whether or not something was an emergency? Who was he to gauge the exact severity of her pain?

And then he'd gone and had the *nerve* to suggest she invest in that extortionate toothpaste bought right out of his very own surgery.

Maybe she should change dentist.

In the supermarket, Angeline navigated the mothers with cartfuls of shopping and skulking children—still in school uniform. Angeline made a beeline for the appropriate section of the supermarket. She uncovered the rows and rows of toothpaste, all laid out there, and she scanned their names, instinctively looking for that nonsense brand: *Blankety White.*

But she couldn't find it.

When she came up for air, realised that she couldn't find it along the shelves of the supermarket, she went in search of a member of staff for some much-needed help. Said member of staff, a boy who couldn't have been much older than fourteen, guided her back along the shelf of the toothpaste and pointed out to her—as if she needed reminding—that there was no tube of toothpaste bearing the name of *Blankety White.*

Trying her best not to bite her tongue from the pain, Angeline thanked him, and then she took the bus back home.

3

LATER IN THE EVENING, Angeline sat in the sitting room of her one-bedroom flat. She slumped on the sofa watching TV, her cat Oxen lying stretched out on her lap. She felt wave upon wave of pain throbbing through her mouth, through her gums, and she couldn't help wondering if—*just maybe*—the tiny little shop which sat on the corner of her road might possibly stock the required toothpaste.

When Angeline hadn't been able to find the toothpaste in the supermarket, she had given up the whole thing as a matter of principle. There just didn't seem much point to it. And she had supposed that the pain would most likely just go away of its own accord.

But it hadn't.

The pain *very much* remained.

She had tried everything, dosed herself up to her eyeballs in painkillers, and it'd just sort of left her with the constant throb at her mouth.

When she felt like she could bear it no longer, Angeline shovelled Oxen off her lap—to many protesting *yowls*—and she got up. She exchanged her slippers for the pair of sturdy boots she always kept by the front door, and she shrugged on a thick, wool-lined coat to cover up her pyjama top. Although Angeline secretly *loathed* those people who thought it appropriate to go out in their pyjamas to public places, she really couldn't muster the strength to put on Real Clothes in her drug-addled state.

In the corner shop, she looked through the various brands of toothpaste, and she noted that there was a whole host of them, all lining the shelves.

But no *Blankety White*.

What was she going to do?

Again, after asking the shop keeper if they might just—*please!*—have a tube of *Blankety White*, Angeline came up short. And, dejected, she returned home.

4

T HAT NIGHT, the throbbing at her jaw kept Angeline awake for the longest time. It kept her awake well into the morning hours, so that Angeline could already see the sun rising up over the horizon when she finally managed to drift off.

Angeline toyed with the idea of not going into work that day—of asking for a sick day—but, in the end, she decided that she would be able to manage.

She got through the day—*just*—and decided on her plan of action.

She headed back to the dentist's office, and managed to make it there by about fifteen minutes past five. The same receptionist was there, of course, though she didn't appear to recognise Angeline from last time . . . then again, Angeline reasoned with herself that, most likely, the receptionist saw hundreds—*thousands?*—of strangers every year, so what would make Angeline so particularly memorable?

"Yes, madam?" the receptionist said.

Angeline pointed out the tube of *Blankety White* yet again and the receptionist removed it from behind the glass case. However, when the receptionist tapped the serial number on the back of the cardboard packaging into her computer, she scowled, hard and wide. She tapped the serial number in again, and then shook her head.

"It seems that we're out of stock," the receptionist said.

Angeline found herself gaping at the cardboard package of *Blankety White* on the counter. "Uh, couldn't I just take *that one?*"

The receptionist, apparently sensing the desperation in Angeline's tone, laid a protective hand on top of the cardboard package. "This one is for display purposes only."

Angeline continued to stare down at the cardboard package.

She could snatch it out from beneath the receptionist's grasp, of that she was certain. The receptionist had to be in her late sixties, no doubt looking to top up her pension. It would be clean, it would be quick.

Angeline just had to pick her moment.

The receptionist turned her attention back down to her computer monitor. "Now, what I *can* do for you is order in . . ."

Angeline made a grab for the cardboard package of *Blankety White.*

The receptionist resisted for a second but she never really got a good hold of the package, and it slipped through her fingertips.

Angeline got paranoid about falling flat on her face, and not managing to escape the dentist's surgery, but now that she had the package of *Blankety White* clutched in her fist, everything seemed to happen so quickly. Everything was much easier.

She barrelled on out through the door, near enough knocking over an old man who was coming in the other direction. Beleaguered, and not sure what to make of the receptionist's shrieks, he simply turned side on and allowed Angeline past.

5

FEELING LIKE A FUGITIVE, Angeline sprinted around the corner—not an easy task given her high heels—and she left the dentist's surgery behind. She felt better immediately when she'd arrived in the car park behind the dentist's surgery.

Like she had gotten away with it.

She tried to think straight, to rationalise just what she'd *needed* to do—that was right she *had* needed to do it . . . there had been no other way that Angeline would've got her hands on a tube of *Blankety White* other than by prising it from the grasp of the clueless receptionist.

But now, now that the adrenalin seemed to be eking its way out of her system, Angeline couldn't help wondering if she really had done the right thing.

She'd *stolen* after all.

Somehow—dizzily—in her mind, before she'd so much as set foot in the dentist's office, she had promised herself that, if it came down to it, she would lay down her cash on the counter, and then snatch the package away. But things had happened so quickly, and she hadn't been able to think things through. And now look where she'd ended up.

A chilly wave passed over Angeline as she thought about how the receptionist had *surely* recognised her from the day before. If not earlier, when Angeline had first entered the dentist's office, then she surely had put two and two together about her when Angeline had rushed on out clutching the tube of *Blankety White*. On her computer, the receptionist had all of Angeline's personal details.

Her name.

Her address.

Her *telephone* number.

Now that Angeline had a chance to think things over, she realised that what she'd just done had been extremely rash, and that she was going to regret it—if she didn't regret it now—in a day or more's time, when she'd finally got herself shot of this troublesome pain.

She glanced about her, tried to make sense of her surroundings, to see if there was a threat bearing down on her. But nobody seemed to be coming. There was no sound of sirens piercing through the air. Surely, though, it was only a matter of time.

They *would* come for her.

Otherwise what sort of a lesson would it teach the rest of society?

Resolved, Angeline trudged out of the car park behind the dental surgery and she headed back up the road where the surgery was located. She stood outside the door for a good couple of moments before she could suck up the strength to step inside.

6

I T WAS MUCH QUIETER within the dental surgery.

There was no sign of the receptionist.

But Angeline could hear her.

When she looked to the waiting room, Angeline saw the old man she had nearly knocked over now sitting down and perusing one of the pristine magazines. He glanced up over his reading material and gave her a cheeky grin.

No doubt that little episode—back there—had been the highlight of his day.

If not the highlight of his week.

Well, at least somebody was getting some sort of enjoyment out of Angeline's plight.

Angeline uncovered the receptionist in the dentist's surgery, she was blabbering on about the whole sorry episode, revealing what had gone on, blow by blow, and demanding that they call the police. When the dentist's gaze drifted over the receptionist's head, to the doorway where Angeline stood, the receptionist too became distracted from her story.

She glanced back at Angeline, and Angeline felt like she had a *fire* brewing in her guts.

"That's . . . that's *her!*" the receptionist said, extending a bony finger.

Angeline found herself staring right at the tip of the finger, and blurring out the surroundings. The pain was now unbearable, and the only way that Angeline could force herself to deal with it was by clamping her teeth shut and shuddering slightly.

But Angeline maintained the presence of mind to reach out to the receptionist, the tube of *Blankety White* still snug in her fist, and offer it back to her.

The receptionist's features gaped wide, and she swivelled about, seemingly asking for permission from the dentist. He simply gave her a nod, and the receptionist relieved Angeline of the tube of *Blankety White*.

Angeline felt her heart sinking slightly as she watched the receptionist shuck out of the dentist's office, and return to her desk. Angeline couldn't help noticing how she had dented the packaging during her escape—she had been holding onto it so tight, as if the tube itself would keep her safe from being discovered.

It hadn't.

Her conscience had seen to that.

The dentist tilted his head to one side, and he crossed his arms over his chest. "Was this all about the recommendation I gave you?"

Angeline nodded, wanting to cry, but staving it off.

The dentist screwed up his eyes and glanced to the side of Angeline's face, to her cheek. He stared intently at some spot that Angeline would've had no chance of seeing without the aid of a mirror. He took a step forwards. Another. And then he stood before her.

He placed his hand on her chin lightly, and swivelled her face so that he could look her dead in the spot which interested him. "That's some pretty nasty swelling, eh?"

Though Angeline was fairly certain that the dentist was only speaking to himself, she answered his question all the same with a nod.

"Give me a second," the dentist said, and he stepped past Angeline, and out into the waiting room.

When the dentist returned, he was smiling lightly. He looked to Angeline and said, "Mr Horrox is willing to wait for a little longer, if you'll let me have another look?"

Feeling somewhat numb, Angeline managed a nod, and then, following the dentist's gesture, she took her place down in the chair. She laid back. And lost herself in the bright swivel light that he adjusted above her head.

7

ABOUT HALF AN HOUR LATER, Angeline walked out of the dentist's office feeling somewhat sore about the mouth, but, on the whole, much better. He had issued her some painkillers to take for the next week or so, and arranged for her to come back for a check-up. He had apologised—*him* apologised to *her*—for not having noticed the issue the day before, but he had mumbled something about not having much time, and feeling a little too rushed to *really* take care. And Angeline had apologised to him for having briefly stolen the tube of *Blankety White*.

In the end, it seemed that things had turned out just fine.

When Angeline got back home, she could no longer feel the throbbing sensation in her cheek, and the drugs the dentist had given her made her sleepy.

And so she flipped on the TV, laid a blanket over her prostate body, and then shovelled her cat Oxen onto her lap.

And, as she lay there, the multi-coloured blur of the TV screen filling her eyes, she found herself drifting away. Her mind flexing and bending. Dreaming. And, when she rose from the sofa in a half-asleep state, to lug herself off to bed, she realised that she had been dreaming about *Blankety White*.

That package, she supposed, would be ingrained on her mind forever.

ONLY PLAYING ALONE

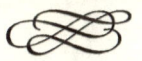

I T'D BEEN A GOOD COMPROMISE, Jackie saw that now.
Yes, she had no regrets about it.

None at all.

Sitting huddled-up in a comfortably collapsing armchair, Jackie stared into the fireplace of her social room at her university halls. The coals were all glowing red-hot, and she drew in the scent of burning coal, down deep into her lungs.

Would that give her cancer later in life?

Well, if it would, then *cancer* be damned!

She could feel the gentle wafting waves of warmth coming off the coal fire, and she could feel it passing right into her blood, warming up her chilly bones. It certainly *had* been chilly back in her dorm room. She supposed the administration turned the thermostat down as low as they could. Most students went home for Christmas at this time of year. But Jackie hadn't. And, from the looks of things, about her halls, she was the only one left here: the one who had stayed behind.

As the heat worked its magic on Jackie, she felt herself dozing a little.

In her mouth, she still had the aftertaste of the hot chocolate she'd prepared about ten minutes ago, before she'd happened upon the brainwave of coming down here to the social room to see if there might be a better prospect of warmth. She hadn't waited for the hot chocolate to cool, that meant she had supped back the near-boiling liquid and singed the roof of her mouth—all the way to her tonsils—in doing so. She drew the woolly blanket she'd pilfered from one of the unlocked storage cupboards up to her throat, and thought about how things might be going off back home . . . what did that word even mean any longer?

Home . . . *home* . . . it sounded somewhat abstract . . . well, that was a bit of a no-brainer considering that it *was* an abstract concept. 'Home' for one person, she supposed, was *hell* for another. And 'home', for what it meant to Jackie, was certainly that:

Hell.

Ever since Jackie could remember, she would have to alternate between her divorced parents' homesteads. Her parents never doing anything lightly, they had set themselves up at opposite ends of the country.

Her mum in the north.

Her father in south.

And Jackie had ended up here—at university—right in the middle.

Each of her parents had found new partners, of course, and the two of them had had their New and Improved families. Her mother had two children: a boy and a girl; while her father had a veritable dynasty with four children . . . all of them boys.

Since Jackie had left school at sixteen, she had ended up staying with friends, paying their families rent for a room from her holiday-time job at a local corner shop in a town not far from the university here. And, since then, Jackie's Christmases would always consist of her going one way, or the other, having to choose where she was going to spend her Christmas.

North or south.

So, this year, she had simply opted out of the decision altogether.

Decided that she would make *no* decision.

She would see out Christmas—and New Year's—here in her university halls.

Alone with her books.

And her holiday TV.

And this wonderful, warming coal fire here.

Jackie had considered whether she should stay with one of her friends over the holidays, but, in the end, she had decided it brought up too many questions. Although she had managed to get herself into such a state of mind that she really couldn't care less about what anybody else thought, she would really rather avoid all those searching questions from well-meaning parents, asking what particular personal tragedy had deprived her of spending Christmas with her 'old folks'.

Nope, Jackie had decided that since she'd got her dorm room for the entirety of the holidays, that she might as well use it as her base for her daytime work at the corner shop. It wasn't too much of a walk to get there from here. Twenty minutes, nothing more.

When Jackie had first come down into the social room this evening, she had been surprised to find that those unbearable, fluorescent strip lights had been turned on full. Her first task, once she had discovered the coal fire, and turned the gas on, had been to turn off those lights. To allow the darkness in. After all, those fluorescent, all-seeing lights really did nothing at all for the aesthetics of the social room. There wasn't all that much to see here.

There were the battered and peeling corkboards, which looked like they'd lived through quite an ordeal, felt the extreme pain of each year from the sixties, when they'd surely been erected, till the present day when they continued to cling to the walls with nothing more than sure willpower and decomposing glue.

It was obvious that the social room had been given several licks of pain down the years. From where Jackie had stood, when she'd first entered, she had been able to make out a patch of wall which had been rubbed away—perhaps due to the nearby chair, and from years and years of leanings—where she counted no less than thirteen different coats.

Among them was a scarlet-red, a navy-blue, before the current fashion had seen the painter-decorators—whoever *they* might be— settle on institutional beige. And, if Jackie had to guess, the social room hadn't been repainted for a good five years, at least. It really *could* do with a lick of paint. She supposed that if she somehow saw her way to becoming unbearably bored she might dig through a storage cupboard and do some painting . . . yeah, like *that* was going to happen.

Jackie hunched her shoulders and lost herself in the gentle, reddish glow of the coals. It was funny, but this—*all this*—was just about as close to paradise as she could remember a Christmas being. She wondered if she could make it last. If her parents would actually fall for the oldest trick in the book, the one which had involved her telling her mother that she was staying at her father's, and telling her father that she was staying at her mother's.

They wouldn't communicate.

They *never* communicated.

Even the briefest, or fleetingest, of mentions of either ex-spouse was certain to generate all sorts of emotional storminess within the appropriate domicile. Both her parents wanted to forget their relationship ever happened. So Jackie had reasoned that also meant them forgetting her too.

That wouldn't be so difficult . . . and Jackie admitted to herself that it might well make things far easier. Make her life more simple.

Strangely, she felt a tear come to the surface of her left eye. But she wiped it away with her palm before it had the chance to fatten and roll down her cheek.

She brought the blankets tighter about herself.

Off, in the near distance, she heard gentle footsteps.

That *scrub* of rubber-soled shoes against coarse hallway carpet.

She turned to look.

And felt a touch of fear.

Jackie knew she must've looked something like a mad woman,

what with her sitting alone, before the coal fire, an old blanket wrapped about her shoulders. But she couldn't quite help that.

In short, she felt just a touch afraid.

She thought through the consequences, about what might happen to her. If she just examined the facts in her mind then it was really quite frightening . . . she was here, she was *alone*, and nobody knew where she was . . . if there was—*indeed*—some sort of a Christmas killer stalking her university halls then it was a fairly sure thing that nobody would find out about till a cleaner uncovered her—*probably violated*—corpse in the second week of January.

But Jackie tried to calm herself down.

Tried to talk her heart around from beating so hard.

She breathed in the familiar scent of the coals.

Absorbed the gentle warmth through her cheeks.

What had shocked her, she speculated later, was that she'd believed herself to be all alone, in her university halls. And now that she found that wasn't the case, it took her somewhat off guard.

She looked to the doorway.

Saw that somebody stood there.

She couldn't make out more than a silhouette.

She decided that she might as well speak up. "Uh, hello?" she said.

The silhouette remained silent long enough to cause a panic to tingle through Jackie's body. But she did her best not to let on. Not to show that this person—*whoever this person was*—had succeeded in frightening her.

She wouldn't play *those* games.

Finally, the silhouette answered.

"All alone here?"

A boy.

A slight accent to his voice.

But pleasant sounding.

A *warm* tone.

Jackie thought on her answer. Thought about all those personal-safety seminars she had gone to in her first week at university, the ones which told her that, if in doubt, she should whip out her mobile and fake a conversation with somebody. But something about this boy—something about his voice—told Jackie she could trust him. That he bore her no ill will.

"Uh, yeah," Jackie finally replied, and then she nodded to the coal fire. "I was just trying to get warm, they must've turned down the heating for the holidays."

"Yes," the boy answered in the affirmative, in that slightly stiff way that non-native speakers do, "I was feeling the same. In my room it is like icicles. I thought . . ."

But his words trailed off, and Jackie was left to pick up the slack.

"Do you," Jackie said, "I mean, would you like to sit here —with me?"

The way she came out with it made her wince ever so slightly. Perhaps she'd been spending too much time alone—too much time with corny Christmas films, listening to all those *corny* lines delivered by doe-eyed actors . . . but what *else* was Jackie supposed to be doing?

The boy shifted out of the doorway. As he approached her, Jackie could gradually make out his features. First she took in his clothing: how he was wearing a pair of three-quarter length trousers, those tracksuit bottoms which all boys seemed to be compelled to use as a sort of 'comfort' wear whenever about the halls. He wore a baggy, black t-shirt over the top half of his square-shouldered frame, and Jackie could see that there was a somewhat smoky image of a wolf howling and a name of a metal band blazing in silver lettering in the foreground.

At least Jackie couldn't imagine that it could be anything *other* than a metal band.

The boy had thick, black eyebrows that seemed to be constantly arched in surprise. His skin had an olive-grey shine to it. When he met her eyes, he flashed her a brief smile and then collapsed down into the armchair which sat beside Jackie's.

He sat slumped back and immediately dipped his hands into the pockets of his tracksuit trousers, apparently for warmth, rather than as any attempt to look cool . . . though Jackie, not being inside of his head, couldn't have been certain.

"Here for the holidays, huh?"

"Yup," Jackie replied, looking away from him and back to the glowing coals.

There was a long silence, but it didn't make Jackie feel uncomfortable. Not in the same way as those silences which often dominated her morning tutorials when the tutor would ask some question about the previous week's reading and it would become evident that nobody had done it.

"Have you no family?" the boy said.

Jackie restrained the urge to grimace at her remark. That was a whole thread of reasoning behind her decision to plonk herself down here in her halls of residence for the duration of the festive period . . . so that she wouldn't have to answer those sorts of questions.

In the end, she decided to simplify things.

"My family's dead."

Jackie held still, feeling both the warmth of the coal fire, and the surely 'oh'-shaped expression which the boy was wearing right then. She had never been a good liar, which was to say that anybody who knew her well enough could read the signs.

The way that she stiffened up whenever she got through with telling one.

The way her voice sometimes cracked when she dished it out through her lips.

This time, though, there was no response from the boy, except for an, "I am sorry to hear of that."

Jackie shrugged. "It's okay," she said, continuing to stare into the coal fire as if she was looking into the middle distance and trying to find some sort of a physical rendering for her interior pain.

As Jackie did continue to stare, she felt the boy's hand reach out for hers, where she'd left her hand on the armrest. Without any further prompting, he gave her fingers a quick squeeze before snatching his hand back. As if he had thought this might be some invasion.

Jackie looked to the boy.

Indeed, as she'd imagined it, he was looking slightly shocked.

A little taken aback.

"I am sorry," he said, "but I do not think." He gave her an uneasy smile, one of those smiles which, Jackie was sure, he had practised countless times in order to ease communication. "Sometimes the British custom, they are, how do you say . . ."

" 'Standoffish' ?"

The boy gave her a squint-eyed glance, but he said, "Yes, something like it, I think."

Jackie rolled her shoulders a little, now feeling a touch of cramp setting in. She supposed that there were some ergonomic issues which went into her slouching about in the armchair before the fire. "I don't know how it happened," Jackie said, "suppose there're some people who still believe that the sun never sets on the British Empire."

"Yes," the boy said, with a slightly furrowed brow. "Yes, that might be."

Another silence opened up between the two of them, and Jackie couldn't help but feeling herself thinking about the lie she had told this boy. How she had basically killed off her own families

—*plural*—in her own mind . . . did that have some sort of signifi-cance, or was it just a silly, throwaway line?

Some demented form of play?

She couldn't quite tell.

"What your name is?" the boy said.

"Jackie."

"Ah. I am Ernesto."

Jackie had to admit that she quite liked the *purr* he gave to the 'r' of his name, and the prompt, definite ending of the 'o'. Some-times Jackie wished she'd been born somewhere else. Somewhere a little more exotic. Somewhere that wasn't so . . . she couldn't really think of how to describe it . . . *straight-laced*?

"Did you see," the boy began, "that outside it is snowing?"

" 'Snowing' " Jackie said, thinking that she *had* been indoors all day, and had hardly bothered to look out the window.

"Yes," the boy said with a nod. "*Snowing.*"

Jackie had never much liked snow.

At best, she found it a minor annoyance.

It seemed to make it so that everything—*especially travel*—took factors longer to get done. Since she'd spent much of her time shut-tling between her mother and father's house for Christmas, she would often find herself at some sort of a backwater village or town, standing on a station platform, jiggling up and down for some sort of warmth. And then there would be a message announced over the PA system, informing passengers for some-service-or-other that a replacement bus service would be offered in lieu of an arriving train.

If Jackie hadn't been so frozen in those moments, then she might've boiled right over.

Now, though, now that she had nowhere to go, she couldn't

help feeling something approaching glee at the prospect. Some sort of childlike wonder. She recalled growing up with her mum. Their house had been some distance from the rest of civilisation— which was just as her mother had liked it—and that had meant none of Jackie's friends, the few of them that there were, would be about to play in the snow with Jackie. She could still remember seeing the snowflakes flutter down outside her windowpane, and how she would venture out—when it was thick enough—and go make a snowman, or *some* snow creature, before returning inside for hot chocolate and marshmallows.

This time things were different.

As Jackie huddled along the hall, Ernesto pacing before her, she couldn't help but feel a slight spark of joy at the base of her gut. She zipped up her coat and shoved her hands into her mittens. When Ernesto reached the door to the outside, he turned around to face her, his eyebrows a little knitted, and said, with a degree of sincerity, "You ready?"

Jackie couldn't help but smile back at him.

There was something about his tone.

Something which made it sound like they might be ready to face off with some life-or-death situation. She wanted to say something to reassure him, something to calm him down, but all she came up with was a slight nod to his question.

Ernesto brought the door to the university halls open, and allowed the creeping, chilling winter air into the place. It did battle with the heating, making Jackie feel, all at once, hot and cold. Her teeth chattered while she felt insanely warm throughout her ribcage and down to her stomach.

Outside, she could make out the bleached-white landscape.

How the snow *had* settled over what had been the concrete spaces outside of their halls of residence. Jackie breathed in deeply, wondering to herself for a moment how she had managed to miss all this. How she hadn't so much as noticed the falling snow.

But she noticed it now.

Ernesto, all wrapped up in his own thick jacket, and with a pair of insulated gloves on his hands, led the way out. She watched as the flakes came unstuck from their brethren, and caught onto the legs of his tracksuit bottoms.

And then, with a smile, and a skip, he ran off.

Into the snow.

~

They must've been out in the snow for hours.

At least, when Jackie noticed the electric lights flickering outside her halls of residence, she could hardly believe all they'd achieved. How they'd managed to do some snow angels, created nothing less than a whole village of snowmen and, now, how they'd put the finishing touches to something which Ernesto referred to in quite vague terms as a 'snow sculpture'.

To Jackie, it simply looked a little like a beehive.

What they'd done to create it had been to roll up a whole series of snowballs, and then pack them all together. Still, she was proud of their work. This *had* been a day in the snow well spent.

It was as she noticed Ernesto shivering, his lips now turned a slight shade of blue, that she felt some compulsion grip her right from the base of the gut. It was almost like she felt a swelling down there. An *irresistible* urge. She reached out and grabbed one of the snowballs off their 'snow sculpture', and, after holding it in her fist for a brief few moments, she wrenched her wrist back and tossed it.

Headshot.

Ernesto flinched at the strike. He wasn't wearing a hat or anything, so she could only imagine how the ice must've felt as it smacked into his skin. Burrowed through his hair. Sent a chill down to the bone. For a second, as he turned to look at her, she saw something approaching anger in his eyes. But it soon evaporated. Replaced by a sneaky smile. He crouched down, shovelled up a fistful of snow, and hurled if back at Jackie.

Missed.

As Jackie ducked away, she went about the task of collecting snow for herself. She lumped it into a mound, packing it together tight, in that way she had always done back at home. When she'd lived with her mother. Preparing those snowballs which she would never have any cause to use.

Not against other children.

Not against her friends.

Only playing alone.

Jackie was too slow, though, and Ernesto had time to form another of his snowballs.

This time he *did* hit her.

In the gut.

A body blow.

Jackie didn't allow it to knock her off balance too long. She pulled herself back together, and readied her aim another time. She wheeled her arm backwards, and then ploughed forwards, feeling the slight chill against the tips of her fingers as she let the snowball go . . . allowed it to arc through the air. And hit her target.

The snowball fight continued for a long while.

Jackie did her best to keep up her munitions, never wanting to find herself outgunned. From what she had discovered thus far, she could tell he was a wily, old character, and so she had to be on her guard. She had to keep her defences well stocked. Nice and protected.

It wasn't till there was nothing but moonlight and the faint glare of the outside lights of the hall that they decided to call it quits.

Just like when she'd been a girl, Jackie felt herself trembling all the way down to the bone. The wind that blew across the snow sent a chill right through her coat, as if it wasn't there at all, and she was glad when she thought of the social room, and how she'd left the coal fire burning away.

It would be like returning to her own personal den.

When they reached the door back into the university halls of residence, though, Ernesto stopped before her. He stood stock still. Apparently distracted by something.

And then, slowly—*gradually*—he turned to face her.

For a long while, Jackie lost herself in his glittering, green eyes, and before she even knew it she felt his warm lips brush up against hers. Just briefly. Just for a moment.

Just a *warming* kiss.

And then it was over and done with.

When they stood apart once more, Ernesto said nothing at all. He only prodded his key into the lock and turned. Allowing them back inside.

Back into the warmth.

Away from the outside chill.

And Jackie realised—without the aid of a mirror—that she was smiling.

Because wherever she was she knew she would always be home.

'Home' was only a state of mind.

BLESS THE BUNNIES

1

FLOYD MAVEKSSON looked out through the large windows over his expansive garden. The lush, green grass. The gentle slope of the hill. His neatly trimmed borders. Those saplings he'd planted not a couple of weeks ago, and which seemed, already, to be thriving, what with their leaves bristling upwards into the air, looking full and virile.

He just *loved* the way the sun glazed his garden at this time of day, the way that it seemed to lift any mean-spirited mood that might've followed him home from the office. Some people went to have massages, others liked to play sport, but for Floyd, the only way that he ever *truly* felt totally and completely—*one-hundred-percent*—relaxed was when he was standing here, in his conservatory, looking out over the garden he had dug out and planted himself.

In many ways, he guessed that it was the very definition of his own Pride and Joy.

And he took any compliment on the verdant state of his garden as personal praise, just as he took any sort of a slight as a personal insult.

The slight, on this occasion, happened to come in the form of rabbits.

Bunny rabbits.

Or, more precisely, the holes that they'd excavated in his otherwise pristine lawn.

As Floyd brought his gaze back from the window, and down to the lawn itself, he caught sight of one of them hopping merrily out from its freshly dug hole.

Floyd stood stock still, not wanting to alarm the rabbit. He stared out through the glass at it. And he waited.

The rabbit sniffed about its feet, about the grass beneath its stodgy body—or was it just extremely fluffy?—and then picked up the trail to the carrot a dozen or so hops away.

Floyd sunk his teeth into his lower lip, anticipating what was going to happen next.

His heart bobbed in his throat.

It seemed that, with each of the rabbit's hops, his blood warmed up another degree.

When the rabbit was only half its body length away from the carrot, its nose protruding out and sniffing at the carrot, Floyd squeezed his fingers into tight fists.

And he waited a little more.

Extra sniffling—around the carrot.

He took in a sharp breath. Felt his heart give another skip. And then, just like that, with no more preamble, the bunny rabbit took a nice, and meaty, chomp out of the carrot.

Floyd squeezed his fingers into fists so tight now that he could feel a wodge of blood seeping into his fingernails. He just about had the presence of mind to glance at his watch. To take note of the time. Then he looked back out again.

The rabbit sniffed around the carrot a little more before taking another few bites. And, soon enough, it had consumed the carrot whole. And looked mightily pleased with itself.

At least it seemed *pleased with itself* to Floyd.

He kept tracking the rabbit, took note of his watch.

Two minutes had passed since the rabbit had taken its first bite.

He felt a fizz through his blood.

He watched the rabbit lollop onwards, up his carefully trimmed border, where it began sniffing at one of his petunias.

Though something inside of Floyd almost compelled him to rush out there, screaming blue murder, he held himself back, forced himself to stand his ground.

He had to be patient now.

Had to take his time.

He could feel his pulse at his temples, battering away there.

The rabbit took a chomp out of one of the petals.

Another chomp.

. . . And then, with a final—extremely *profound*—chomp, it promptly flopped over on its side and lay still.

Dead still.

Floyd relaxed.

He grinned.

At last, he had put the Rabbit Issue to bed.

Once and for all.

2

THAT AFTERNOON, Floyd found himself helping out his wife Hillary in the kitchen.

They were baking blueberry muffins in the kitchen . . . well, to be a little more accurate, *Hillary* was baking blueberry muffins while Floyd sat at the kitchen table, the weekend newspaper spread before him, and the sun beaming down across his back.

He also had a nicely poured pint of ale sitting before him of which he had already gulped down a steady half.

As he scanned the cricket scores from the day before, Floyd reached across and took hold of his pint glass. Brought it to his lips. Drank in that sour—yet smoothly satisfying—taste. He couldn't help but smack his lips as he laid the glass back down on the kitchen table with a glassy *thunk*.

He removed his reading glasses from his face, laid them down across the opened newspaper and then reclined in the hard-backed, wooden chair he sat on.

He folded his hands and rested them behind his head, and breathed in the rich odour of the cooking muffins.

As he watched Hillary open up the oven door, to check on the golden-brown muffins nestled inside, he thought that he might push his luck.

This *had* been a wonderful day, after all.

He *might as well!*

"D'you think," he began, "I could possibly . . ."

Oven-gloved and aproned, Hillary removed the freshly baked tray of muffins from the oven and then glanced back over her shoulder. She gave him one of her signature scowls. "They'll be here in ten minutes, can't you wait? Or are you some sort of a perpetual toddler?"

Floyd couldn't help but grin at the remark.

That was the gal he'd fallen in love with.

He loved how she really knew how to take a bite—how, despite her white hair, and her wrinkled face, she still packed that same venom with a lash of her tongue.

And she wasn't afraid to dish it out either.

Feeling good from the ale, feeling that confident warming feeling right down to the base of his gut, Floyd took a chance. "Think that a perpetual toddler would've been able to sort out the Rabbit Issue?" He even made bunny ears with his fingers as if to emphasise his success.

Hillary slipped off her oven gloves and, with a clean fork, plucked from the drawer, she punctured the surface of one of the muffins, brought up coils of steaming flavour. She gazed at the prongs of the fork as she withdrew, giving it a stoical look of approval.

She glanced back at Floyd briefly before she began to untie the knot of her kitchen apron. When she spoke to him, she had already turned her back to him. "You and those rabbits—never give it a rest, do you?" She plodded over to the oven and hung her apron up there. "Anybody else'd be happy to have some company out there, in the garden, to stop them feeling so lonely."

Lonely!

Floyd almost spurted out a geyser of the ale he'd just supped at.

He grinned to himself as he swallowed the ale down, shaking his head lightly, wondering to himself about how *anybody*—anybody keen on gardening—could foster any sort of a liking, let alone *fondness*, for a common pest.

Hearing a car engine off in the near distance—Floyd was *extremely* proud of how well he had preserved his hearing in his old age—he hoiked himself up, sucked up the dregs of his ale, and then placed the emptied glass in the sink.

On his way to the front door, he risked a swooping kiss to Hillary's cheek.

He managed to hit his target, though she attempted to take evasive action.

Her skin, as he always thought to himself—and how he'd *never* say out loud . . . for obvious reasons—was like brushing up against a sun-warmed peach.

As he made his way down the hallway, off to answer the door, he heard Hillary's voice follow him. "And why's it that you're in such a blooming great mood? You usually *hate* it when they come by to visit. It's like you've found a plant that magically produces ale."

But, as Floyd came closer to the front door, he didn't even allow this particular sideswipe in. He simply ignored it.

Because he had solved a problem that had wracked his existence for countless weeks.

3

T HEY SAT OUT in the back garden: Floyd's son Joe, his wife Emma—today wearing a low-cut white top which exposed her *ample* snow-white bosom—and their two-year-old son, and three-year-old daughter. Floyd's *grandchildren*.

As Floyd sipped at his ale, and aimed what must've been his sixth, or *seventh*, pass over Emma's cleavage, he couldn't help but breathe in the sweet air—the smell of the roses, and the pine trees, and the gentle odour of the lawn all around them.

The birds twittered in the trees, and though it wasn't a completely pristine—*blue-skied*—day, those soggy-bottomed clouds were holding off, staying in their place off at the edge of the horizon on the fields.

Yes, today *really* wasn't far at all from being perfect.

As Floyd leaned back a little more on his green, plastic garden chair, he reached up to shade his eyes from the sun, and he looked to his boy . . . his grown-up boy, Joe . . . two kids, a wife . . . how had that happened so quickly?

Floyd smiled at Joe and said, "Everything going well at the company?"

Today Joe wore a light, cream-coloured shirt with the sleeves rolled back up to his elbows. He had on a pair of sunglasses that seemed to wrap themselves all the way up to cover his eyebrows.

Why anybody would want to shield their *eyebrows* from the sun, Floyd didn't really have much of an idea.

But, then again, he supposed, it was all the rage these days to cover up when it got sunny . . . skin cancer, and all that.

Joe tilted his head to one side and he reached for his glass of lemonade which sat on the table before him. He clutched hold of it, and replied, "Yes, everything's fine—*busy*, but all going fine."

"Good, good," Floyd said, going for his seventh—or was it

eighth?—pass of Emma's cleavage. Out of politeness, he looked to Emma now and asked her some question or other about the babies . . . to be quite honest, he forget about the question pretty much the second that it left his lips, but she answered him with a standard, "Very well," and smiled a lot, so he supposed that he had fulfilled his social nicety.

They sat in silence for a long while till Hillary appeared—bearing the tray of blueberry muffins—and set the tray down on the table between them. She hovered for a few seconds before, with his glance, Floyd managed to cajole her to take a seat with them.

Even then, though, she remained perched right on the edge of the chair, as if something pressing might occur at any second.

Floyd was always trying to help her get out of this *highly-strung* intense hosting personality of hers. But, the fact remained, she was barely capable of remaining still.

They'd all got their muffins, and a plate to go with it, and were chomping along quite nicely when Floyd's grandson, Dwayne, came toddling up to his side.

Like always, Dwayne had a dribbling nose, and if Floyd had been of that bent, he might've reached into his pocket and wiped away the mucus with a handkerchief. But, since he found both children and handkerchiefs repulsive in equal measure, he simply smiled down at the boy, wearing a pair of dungarees and with an inquisitive expression smeared over his face. "Bunnies," Dwayne said.

"Hmm?" Floyd replied, still grinning, but also sneaking off a glance to the boy's parents. Children's expressions always perplexed him. It seemed almost like a secret code, like there was a whole bunch of English-language manipulation that simply flew right over Floyd's head.

At the present moment, however, both Joe and Emma were indulged in conversation with Hillary.

So it seemed that Floyd would have to do his best to comprehend the boy.

" 'Bunnies' ?" Floyd said, his smile now seeming to tug at the corners of his mouth.

Dwayne nodded his head, his lips slightly parted and that line of mucus sparkling in the sunlight. And then, just like that, he turned and toddled on, across the garden.

Floyd sat back in his chair, reached out for his ale, and brought it to his lips. Right as he was about to drink, he heard Hillary's chiding tone break through the conversation on the other side of the table. "He wants you to follow him," she said.

Floyd set his pint back down on the table, gave his wife a slightly beleaguered glance and then he lifted himself up out of his chair.

Children were exhausting.

There was a certain truth to that.

Thank *God* he and Hillary had only had the one.

Floyd picked his way across his lawn, past his granddaughter— Emily—and continued on after Dwayne.

Dwayne toddled on, seeming, to Floyd, like he was making a beeline for his flowerbed, where he, no doubt, was about to show Floyd how he'd been merrily stomping the petunias that he'd spent all last week planting.

However, thankfully, Dwayne stopped short of the flowerbed, got down on his haunches in that improbable, physics-bending way that toddlers do, and, with a hand smeared with dried-up bogies, he pointed at the turf.

Over Floyd's shoulder, there was a peal of laughter.

He glanced back at the table.

They all had their backs to him.

Somehow Floyd always got it into his head, whenever his son came to visit, that he and Hillary would be laughing about him for something or other.

Perhaps he was paranoid, or perhaps—*just perhaps*—he was onto something.

"Bunnies," Dwayne said again.

Floyd turned to look. He followed the boy's index finger.

To the stirred earth, to the earth that he had used to fill in that ill-fated rabbit's hole—the rabbit that he had dealt the poisoned carrot this morning.

Floyd screwed up his eyes and stalked closer to the boy. He glanced down, over Dwayne's shoulder, and into the hole, where, inside, all clustered-up together, nothing much more than a bundle of white fur.

Baby bunnies.

4

THANKFULLY, Dwayne turned out to be more interested in looking out through the chain-link fence, and across the field which ran behind the house, than gazing down into the hole stuffed full of bunnies.

All the while, as Floyd guided his grandson about the perils of the long grasses that ran beside the fence to the field, he found his mind stuck on the bunnies, and what he would do to them. Those bunnies, the ones in the rabbit hole which Dwayne had uncovered, they were surely the offspring of that bunny from this morning. And so it followed that they'd grow up to be adult bunnies—adult bunnies who would chomp at his carefully cultivated garden.

Yes, there was no doubt about it.

The bunnies needed to go.

But how?

He didn't have any poison left over.

He had really dosed that carrot up this morning with pretty much all he could get his hands on. He hadn't wanted to take any chances. Hadn't wanted to waste more than one carrot.

So, to his mind, that left two distinct options . . . *three* really, if he thought about it.

The easiest, and perhaps the option with the greatest random factor, would be for him to fill in the hole of the bunnies and trust, to the hand of fate, that they couldn't dig themselves out again . . . of course, that was with the hope that not one of the bunnies *would* dig a hole back out again and, to tell the truth, he really hadn't much knowledge about bunnies and at which particular stage of their maturity they started *burrowing*.

The other two options—the most *effective* options—would be far more hands-on.

He could either drown them, or snap their little bunny necks.

As he strode along, through the long grasses, he felt Dwayne's tiny, fragile hand brush against his fingertips. It took hold of Floyd's fingers tightly, using him to support his weight. "Go back?" Dwayne said, apparently wanting Floyd to bring him back to his mother and father.

Floyd risked a final glance over his shoulder, out across the fields, and he couldn't help feeling that slight—*ever so slight*—clench of his heart at the thought of having to off all those little bunnies. But, as he reminded himself, little bunnies turned into *big* bunnies.

And big bunnies created *Issues*.

As Floyd approached the table, the muffins now all eaten save for two or three, which he would eat himself later on, he noticed his son looking at his wristwatch, giving a slight yawn, and then giving his wife a sidelong glance . . . then a barely discernible nod.

Hillary was wittering on about something or other, in that way she did, apparently unaware that she had long ago lost the attention of her captive audience.

Floyd peeled back his lips with a smile, still holding onto Dwayne's hand.

As they got closer still, Dwayne released Floyd's hand and, with a cry of "Mummy!" rushed into his mother's waiting arms.

Floyd, actually a little worn out by all this osmosis parenting, slumped down in his chair where he was pleased to find a good half of his glass of ale remaining.

He took it down him in one.

As he replaced the glass on the table, he overheard Emma speaking with Dwayne, in that obnoxious, motherly way—the way mothers use their offspring as a sort of buffer for a conversation with living, breathing adults.

"Where've you been then?"

Dwayne, of course, just babbled something.

"What's that?" she said, grinning inanely.

Floyd turned his attention back to the fields, and to the golden sunlight which layered across the wheat blowing back and forth in the gentle late-afternoon, early-evening breeze.

" 'Bunnies' ?" she said, apparently emulating Dwayne's garbled phrasing.

Then she looked up at Floyd with a confused expression. "What does he mean?" she said. "I didn't know you had bunnies."

Before Floyd could pitch in with a reply, Hillary spoke for him. "Killed a bunny this morning, did Floyd."

Emma, apparently, judging by her open-mouthed gape, was appalled by this. "What?"

Hillary flashed her eyebrows at Floyd. "Poisoned it."

Emma turned on Floyd, perhaps for the first time that day directly addressing him. "But why?" she said, a slight gasp chasing her words along.

Floyd gave a shrug and turned his attention back to his blossoming and blooming garden. "Pests," he said. "Kill everything in their path."

Emma turned her attention back to Dwayne, slumped on her lap and looking just a little dopey . . . maybe he needed to take a nap or something. "Well, we love animal-waminals, don't we?"

Floyd rolled his eyes at this, and looked over at his granddaughter, Emily, still playing out her silent game with her dolls on the lawn. He wondered just how these kids would turn out at the end of everything. Would they grow up to be a pair of softies?

. . . All kids seemed to these days.

It was an inevitability.

Just then, as if the thought had only just occurred to Emma, she snapped her neck up and looked over at Hillary. "He didn't"—she met Floyd's eye for brief second—"I mean, you *didn't* . . . show him the dead rabbit, did you?"

Floyd thought about how to respond to this and, in the end, decided that the truth was just a little less complicated. He jerked his thumb off in the direction of his lawn, the direction of the hole with the baby rabbits. "No, we uncovered a rabbit hole back there, a whole bunch of babies in it—guess they must be the bunnies of the rabbit I offed this morning."

Emma's eyes widened. She looked about the whole table as if she was too afraid to say anything more.

Floyd suppressed a sigh, already double guessing his wisdom at having revealed the existence of the bunnies because now—surely —there was going to be a whole bunch of resistance coming his way. And he could really just do with being left alone to do as *he* saw fit.

"Yeah," Floyd said, deciding that he couldn't really stop now, "I'm going to take care of them later—when you've all gone off home."

" 'Take care of them' *how?*" Emma asked.

Floyd looked from Joe's face to Hillary's, saw those warning expressions there, telling him that he'd better watch how he stepped next.

But, and maybe it was a little of that lingering joy from the morning, at having taken care of Mummy Bunny, Floyd felt that familiar warmth in his chest as he turned his hand over and inspected his fingernails. "Drown them, probably."

" *'Drown'* them!" Emma said.

Floyd felt a certain tightness enter the air, a sort of friction spring up between everybody sat around the table. When he looked to Dwayne, his lip wobbled, and then, as if his mother had flipped a switch, he broke out into warbling tears.

Emma cupped her hands about Dwayne's ears and drew him to her breast. She pursed her lips as she mumbled soft nothings to him.

Joe looked over the table to Floyd and said, "Well, guess we'd better be getting a move on, hmm?"

Floyd rose from his own chair, looked back over to Emily.

Saw that she'd gone.

Disappeared from sight.

He blinked a couple of times, turned his attention back to the table, and then said, "Yes, I suppose you should be."

Joe glanced about, while Emma continued to salve Dwayne. "Have you, uh, seen that girl of mine anywhere about here?"

Floyd blinked a couple of times, and then said, "I guess she's gone off wandering in the garden. Come on, let's go and have a look."

Right as Floyd and Joe were leaving the table behind, leaving Hillary and Emma behind, he overheard Hillary offering them the remainder of the muffins 'to take home' and, much to Floyd's consternation, he heard Emma accepting.

It seemed that there wouldn't be any muffins for a late-night snack . . . not unless Hillary saw her way to baking another batch . .

.

5

THEY FOUND EMILY crouched over the rabbit hole, the same one which Dwayne had earlier uncovered, and within which were located the bunny babies, all of them fluffy and white, and—to a certain eye, Floyd supposed—*cute*.

Floyd stood back from Joe as he got a look down the rabbit hole, got a look down at the bunnies nestled within. When Emily glanced upwards, with wide eyes—though he knew absolutely nothing about child psychology, didn't really *want* to know anything about it either—he knew precisely what she was going to say.

"Can we take one home, Daddy?" she said.

Joe slipped Floyd and uneasy look. "Uh, I don't think there's any space at home," he said, and then looked back at Emily, who was now stroking the back of one of the bunnies. "Come on," he continued, "I think we'd better be making tracks."

But Emily wouldn't shift from where she crouched.

She simply continued to stroke the bunny's back.

Floyd looked beyond them, out to the fields which ran along the back of the house. *God*, how he would love to just jump the fence and go running through there . . . at the very least he would be alone . . . and able to deal with this newly arrived Rabbit Issue.

"Daddy?" Emily said, in that extremely annoying, and *high-pitched* way that young girls can ask questions.

Joe scratched the back of his neck, looked about him, as if an answer would be floating by on the air, and then he glanced back at Floyd. "You, uh, haven't thought of keeping them *here*, have you?"

Floyd felt a tightness in his chest. He was fairly certain of just where this was heading—just where this line of questioning was heading . . . and he didn't like it . . . not one bit.

But he didn't have a chance to answer, because, just then, Emily called out for her mother, and by extension Dwayne and Hillary, to come and take a look.

Floyd could feel a sweat break out on the surface of his skin. It sent a prickling sensation flushing through his nerves. But there was no stopping it now—it was like a boulder had been sent skittering down a hillside and it brought a whole storm of chunks of rock and stone with it in its trail.

And so Floyd found himself enduring all the bunched-up *oohs!* and *aahs!* as his family took in the baby bunnies nestled in the hole. And while they 'certainly couldn't' take one of these bunnies home with them, they kept on directing questions to Floyd about how they'd love to come and see them when they visited next month.

Floyd did his best to be non-committal.

But even *he* wasn't convinced by his own efforts.

And so it ran, with his family—*finally*—becoming bored with looking at the screwed-up little bundles of fluff and scarpering off to their people-carrier car and trundling off down the road, away from the house.

As Floyd stood there, on his front doorstep, smiling and waving his family off, he listened in on Hillary . . . well, he didn't have much choice since she was chattering right into his ear. "I'll get a cardboard box, shall I?"

"A cardboard box for what?" Floyd said, still smiling and waving at the departing family. "For all the little bunny bodies?"

Hillary didn't answer that question. She only gave him an acute nudge in the ribs.

When the car slipped from sight, Hillary returned inside the house, while Floyd stood there in the porch, wondering just how this had all played out, how he'd found himself in this situation . . . but there seemed little to nothing that he could do about it . . . for now.

6

LATER THAT EVENING, Floyd finished his dozenth ale for the day and he found himself trudging—a mite sleepily—on out to the garage.

As he dug about in the dusty and cobweb-strewn cupboard where he kept his bottles of ale, he heard a slight scuffling from over his shoulder.

When he turned and looked, he spied the cardboard box there, a couple of tufts of straw sticking out from the top. The condition on keeping the bunnies—as he'd agreed it with Hillary—was that she would be the one to look after them . . . she would be the one to feed them, clean them out, etcetera, etcetera, etcetera . . . and if they got too big, no *when* they got too big then they'd search out some appropriate homes for them . . . the 'appropriate' part of that clause had been of Hillary's making.

But now, his hand gripping tight to a bottle of ale, Floyd couldn't help but find himself standing over the cardboard box, staring on down at those . . . and even he had to admit it, no matter how much it stung . . . *cute* bunny rabbits within.

He watched them: pink eyes, white fur, scuffling about, rubbing up against one another.

He glanced about himself, into the shadows of the garage as if Emma herself might've waited behind to witness such a moment, such a time to tell him 'I told you so'.

But, of course, Floyd was alone.

He stuck his bottle of ale beneath his arm, and reached down.

Gently, his fingers hardly making contact, he stroked their fluffy backs. And he felt a strange thrill pass through his bones. An almost *gushing* warm feeling. And, just like that, he found himself smiling—smiling wide and being unable to stop.

Then, just like that, he felt a tear snake its way down his cheek.

A single tear.

He wiped it away with his palm, then wiped his palm on his trousers as if it was a dirty thing.

Still smiling away, with a final look at the bunnies, he replaced the lid on the cardboard box and headed on back to the house.

When he sat down at the kitchen table, sat down to watch Hillary soaping up the dishes and giving them a good scrub, he couldn't help but feel his mind filling with those bunnies, with all those fluffy *white* bodies . . . and that ticklish feeling . . . what could he call it—was there a name?

He guessed that *happiness* was something of a blunt concept, batted about *far* too often. But that was what he would have to settle on.

Happiness it was, then.

No other way to describe it.

He was *happy*.

BACK IN TOUCH

H OT MILK spurted on out of the machine. Sent billowing clouds up into the air. Layered yet more condensation onto the insides of the windows. It smelled sour—sour enough to turn my stomach. But I busied myself with the taste of the all-too bitter coffee I cradled between my fingers.

I laid the coffee cup down onto the laminated, sticky brown surface of the table, and then dropped the silver and foam-stained spoon inside of it with a slight *clink*.

The warmth from the boiling water on the other side of The Seabrudge Café counter came at me in waves. Dampened my skin with sweat.

I thought about what I was doing, and *why* I was doing it . . . I really didn't come up with any plausible explanations.

I was wearing a long, beige jacket which covered up the light blue summer dress which I wore underneath. Though it was September, we'd yet to hit that turning point in the evenings—the point when the breeze carries a chill to it and makes wearing trousers all but compulsory.

But I'd still worn the jacket all the same.

Just in case.

Just in case the weather *did* turn on the long walk back home.

I had decided to tie my sleek black hair back into a bun in a way that kept it out the way . . . out of sight, out of mind . . . and I'd dabbed on just a spot of perfume: this vanilla-smelling stuff that I got one Christmas years ago from some auntie or acquaintance.

We'd been talking about getting back in touch for a long while: me and Matthew. We'd got on email, got talking. But it was different—just completely *unimaginably* different—to actually meet up again. A bolt from the blue.

And it was funny that I only really realised the fact sat there, in that dingy, half-dilapidated train station café, waiting for him, just as I'd always seemed to be doing in the five years of our relationship.

To occupy myself, I gazed on out of the window. Past the murky condensation. Onto the grimy train track: deserted for now, apparently between trains, looked to the sleek, shining rails, and then a little further to the downtrodden foliage which seemed to have been flattened into a very final—very *dead*—brown.

A chain-link fence ran about the compound of the train station, and though there was barbed wire coiled about the top of it, I couldn't really see why anyone would want to climb.

There was only grim, concrete buildings beyond.

Or maybe it was the other way around.

Maybe they wanted to stop those from the outside getting *in* . . .

I turned my attention back to the inside of the café, to the sad little booths: the moulded plastic *brown* booths with the table in the middle, and then the plastic benches at either side—hardly large enough to seat more than one person, though I could see a family off in the corner of the café, five of them: a mother, a father, two boys, and a girl, all squidged in the best they could.

It was funny, maybe what attracted me to the family was the behaviour of the children. The way that they were all so *well* behaved. Not *one* of them so much as kicked their heels as they sat there, tucking into their biscuits, blowing on their steaming mugs of hot chocolate.

I wondered if they were tired.

If they'd come a long way.

And they were simply exhausted.

. . . Or perhaps the parents were *strict* . . . it's funny the things that the eye *can't* see.

I looked to the father. He wore a cream shirt webbed with

brown lines. And he had a moustache, slightly stubbly cheeks, and bright eyes. Though from where I sat, I couldn't make out the colour, I was almost certain that they were brown . . . that kind of *hazel*-brown shade.

The mother wore a simple V-necked t-shirt, tucked into the waistband of her blue jeans. She had short blond hair, cropped in a boyish way so that it only tickled the very tops of her pearly ears.

When she caught me looking, I glanced away.

Turned my attention back out the window.

Back to my waiting.

. . . But she didn't catch me looking before I'd had an opportunity to take in the children.

And how they all looked like just about the most *perfect* children.

All of them wearing thick, woolly jumpers.

Those cherubic, pouched cheeks.

Their gently blinking eyes, still dazed at the wonder of the world . . . I wondered if mine and Matthew's children might've been like that . . . or if they would've been a disaster.

As I glanced to the counter of the café, I caught the eye of the forty-something lady who ran the place. She had puffed-out, heat-inflicted red cheeks. All mixed in with that kind of pale complexion that makes you know *instantly* that the person works in a hot environment.

Spends a good portion of the day sweating it out.

. . . At least *I've* always been able to notice those types of people.

She had tufty black hair that seemed to be on the cusp of turning to a bluish grey. Her body was boxy, perhaps beaten up by several pregnancies. The slightly stained white overalls she wore seemed to almost be symbolic of her virginity stolen many times over . . . and, well, look at me, getting all dewy-eyed again, getting all emotional about the world . . .

It was with a dull *tinkle* of that sad, beaten-up brass bell which hung over the door that brought my attention to him.

To Matthew.

Walking into the café.

And back into my life.

After all these years.

Romeo He Ain't

I LOVE THOSE MOMENTS—the moments when you go to meet someone and you see them before they see you. It's like a tiny window onto a person's private life: a brief glimmer of just who they really are.

I never did find out who Matthew really was.

I took him in for as long as I dared. Absorbed his gunmetal-grey jacket which swooped on down right to the balls of his ankles. Took in the way he wore his mousy-brown hair side-parted, with a little gel. I also saw that coin-sized bald patch emerging at the pinnacle of his skull. And I wondered if that was a clue, if that was maybe something to keep tucked away for later on . . . it might turn out to be useful, after all.

His nose, constantly squashed from, apparently, according to Matthew, a playground fight where he'd got the better of some other kid . . . though I've reason to believe, from those conversations with his mother, back when we'd go on visits to her retirement home, that Matthew was far more likely to have been the bullied, than the bully at school.

It seemed like the air of the café got to him straight away, because I could already see the slight sheen to his skin, the way the perspiration was leaking out of him.

He glanced about the café.

His eyes cast about to the corner.

To the same family *I* had inventoried . . . and then he fixed his eyes on *me*.

For a long second I lost myself in those deep blue eyes of his, felt myself plunging down into their cool depths. Falling into the no-doubt clear and fresh water there. Breathing in his musky scent all over again.

And, just like that, the moment was gone.

The woman at the counter of the café calling away his attention.

Matthew gave me the briefest of smiles, gave the lady his order, along with an awful lot of nodding and smiling, and then he sauntered over to my table.

My chest felt prickly all of a sudden.

And I was certain that this was wrong.

But I made no move.

Matthew could make the move.

He drew a deep, deep breath. His eyes still wading over mine. And his shoulders heaved back in an almighty inhale, then he breathed out.

And I sensed all those things. The stale sweat. The slight odour of exhaust. Hours-old deodorant . . . and, a little way beyond all the rest, I detected also *his* smell, the one that I had breathed in every day, and every night as we lay in bed together.

Before I really had a chance to gather myself together, he swooped down on me, gave me a kiss on the cheek, his stubble grating against my skin, rubbing against me as if it was sandpaper.

When he straightened up, dropped himself down onto the plastic bench opposite mine, he was grinning: long and hard, his jagged charming teeth just as I remembered them.

Just as sharp.

It was only then that I noticed he was carrying a briefcase—but of course he was. It was one of those which folded out, like an accordion, though now it was currently clasped tight. It was brown in a way that, I supposed, was meant to compliment the grey jacket he wore . . . and, for the first time in our meeting, I got that unpleasant *pang* in my gut, that whoever it was who'd picked out this jacket and briefcase combo, it wasn't Matthew.

He had never really had a sense of style.

Never really had any time for it, truth told.

Still grinning, Matthew straightened himself up on the bench.

He smartly tugged his jacket off his shoulders to reveal the crease-less white shirt he wore underneath. He'd also knotted himself into a light purple, diamond-patterned tie.

He wore long sleeves, but he reached down and undid the buttons.

I saw that his fingers were shaking slightly.

And I caught a whiff of his sour sweat once again.

Once he had rolled his cuffs up to his elbows, he took me in. His eyes smiling just as much as his mouth did, but those dark circles which surrounded them suggesting that he was a haunted man . . . that he was a *pursued* man . . . or perhaps a *condemned* man . . . a man who would not be pinned down, in any case.

"So," he said, sinking back into the plastic bench, slipping just a little, but keeping himself balanced using his elbows as a crutch on the table, "guess you got my message."

I gave him a smile. It seemed so *weird* to be *smiling*: here and now, with everything that had gone between us . . . but, then again, *why not?*

"I, uh," Matthew began, his smile straightening out just a touch as he checked his watch—golden, and gleaming in the fluorescent lights of the café—"I've got about half an hour till my train leaves."

I studied the timbre of his voice. Wondered if there was anything different about it. Whether or not he'd acquired a certain weariness to his tone . . . or maybe he was just tired.

He *had* been travelling all day after all.

I dipped my eyes. Turned my attention to my emptied coffee cup before me. The sad little undrunken black-brown pool at the bottom of it, and the jaundice-yellow marks on the silver spoon.

For some reason I just couldn't speak. It felt like my throat had clear dried up. Like my tongue was about as much use as a sponge which had been left out to bleach in the sun.

I waited out the ticks of my heart.

Tried to compose myself.

But Matthew saved me.

He spoke again.

"How've you been?" he said.

I kept my eyes downwards. Now choosing to focus on my dainty fingers, and the subtle coat of clear varnish I'd painted onto my fingernails that morning.

When I dared glance upwards, I noticed Matthew staring at my fingernails.

I managed a smile, and something approaching a nod. "Fine," I said. "You know, just like always . . . things, just as they should be."

Matthew nodded along, an idiotic grin threatening to break out on his lips. But he kept it just about locked away inside of himself. Never allowing it quite to pass his jagged teeth. He glanced off into the corner, back to that perfectly-behaving family. When he spoke, he spoke out of the corner of his mouth. "*Painting* still going, is it?"

I felt my stomach contract slightly. A pulse of blood jarred upwards—into my brain. But I kept myself still. *Thought* I kept myself from showing any outward signs . . . or maybe I was just fooling myself.

". . . Yeah," I said.

"Mm," Matthew said.

I noticed, over his shoulder, the lady who ran the café carrying a cup of black coffee. She set it down between us, between Matthew's sprawled hands. Then, with a professional smile, turned her attention to me—to my emptied coffee cup. "Get you something else?" she said.

I shook my head.

She gave another smile, a nod, then she lifted up my coffee cup —the silver spoon jangling as she made her way back to the counter. Back to her milk steamer, and her coffee machines, and those sickly sweet treats she kept behind glass.

Matthew tore open the packet of sugar which had arrived on

the dish served with the coffee. Then he stirred the sugar in with his silver spoon.

I watched that coal-black mass all swilling, all congealing as he did so.

Back when we'd been together, I'd always admonished him about putting far too much sugar into the stuff he ate . . . I mean, he would put it into *everything* . . . once I even caught him sugaring a glass of water.

Now, though, he was free of my regime.

Out of *my* chains, and into *another's*.

When Matthew had finished up with his sugar-stirring routine, he held his coffee cup up to his lips, blew across the surface, and sent steam swilling into the air. He took a sip, winced—I suppose at the temperature rather than the taste—and then he set the cup back down onto the table before him.

He blinked several times, his smile now gone. His expression dour once more.

Dour in that same way it would get sometimes when we were together.

His eyes somewhere far off.

Then, ever so slowly, they came back to me.

His eyes locked onto mine, and he said, "At home—I'm . . . not *happy*."

A S IF he'd just hit some sort of a trigger—something that he hadn't been intending to reveal at all—he looked away from me . . . looked back to that family in the corner of the café.

Again, I waited out the beats of my heart. Waited out the numbness that rippled through my nerves, and seemed to make my lungs prickle.

I stole a glance back to the counter, to the lady there, busying herself with an array of glasses which she kept stacked all along the back, all of them shining-clean, and yet, at the same time, all bathed in the steam from the churning milk frother.

Matthew stared into the abyss of his black coffee.

I wondered what he was going to say next.

If he *was* going to say anything more.

Or if he was simply going to wait out the minutes till his train left, give me a polite nod, and then shove off along the platform . . . grey jacket draped about his shoulders, briefcase clutched firmly in his large, bloodless hands.

My heart skipped a beat. I never thought about what I was doing. I simply reached across the table. My well-moisturised hands skidding off the varnish. And I found his own. Found the nooks and crevices of his hands—the callouses and the notches, those hands which had once been so important, which had once been so sure and firm . . . like a safety net that would keep me from falling, something that would keep me *connected* to this world, and away from the void of the next . . .

Our fingers entwined. My heart calmed. My blood cooled. And I could feel a slight ringing sound begin in my ears.

He looked away from his coffee, met my eyes once again, and said, his voice shaking a little, "I'm so . . . glad . . . we could do *this*."

For a brief second I had the urge to break out into laughter. To take in The Seabrudge Café one more time, and to heave my head back and laugh my face off . . . that this was just about the *last* location in the entire world for a, potentially, romantic engagement.

But I kept myself under control.

Knew that I owed it to myself, and to Matthew, to keep my emotions in check.

Whether they be jubilation or despair.

He squeezed my hands tighter.

I looked into his eyes and said, ". . . So?"

Matthew breathed in deeply. I watched as his cheeks filled with air and then emptied just as quickly. He glanced about himself then fixed himself back onto my gaze. "I . . . I don't think I can *do* it anymore."

"Do *what?*" I said, only now realising that the conversation had dropped to the level of a whisper, as if we were co-conspirators . . . as if we *both* had as much to lose in this encounter.

"My life," he said, "it's just nothing like how I thought it would be." His focus slipped to the steamed-up window, to a train that was shuttling along the platform, making that whispering *hiss* as it rushed on by. Even when the train had gone, he kept on staring out there, out across the bare tracks. "And, you know, that was when I was thinking—thinking about *us*, and how . . . well, the last time that I really knew what I was doing, knew sort of where I was in my life, was back when we were together."

He continued to look out the window as if his words were for the train tracks rather than for me.

I stared at his face in profile. Saw the way that what had once been a chiselled jawline—or had I just imagined it that way?—had given way to stodgier skin . . . much looser, flubbery skin.

I knew, having to look at myself in the mirror every morning, that I had only grown thinner. That *my* features had become more *severe*—as I recall one of my mentors once describing them . . . and if it hadn't been while I'd been sitting for him while he painted then I might well have given him a good throttling.

No, now we were different people.

When we had parted we'd shot off in opposite directions at maximum velocity.

I could still feel him squeezing my hands with his own, in that slightly terrified way that a child might instinctively grab for his mother's hand.

A safety net.

But he knew better than that.

I could never be *anyone's* safety net.

He snapped back to me. His eyes seemed a little clearer now. Less like he was staring into some haze, trying to make out indistinct forms within it . . . no, he was beginning to peel back the layers and cut to the quick, to get to see what it was that he'd come here looking for in the first place: memories.

"Please," he said, his throat sounding dry, his voice cracked.

I thought back to those giddy moments. They seemed so long ago sat there. When I'd been absent-mindedly taking a well-won break, and I'd been sitting in my kitchen in my creaky little one-bedroom terraced house just five minutes away from the train station, five minutes away from The Seabrudge Café where we sat now.

How my mobile had buzzed.

How I'd seen those words all etched out in the message:

Meet me at the station. I'll be there in an hour. M x

I could've just ignored the message. What would've happened then? No doubt Matthew would've just waited about for the hour till his connecting train came along . . . and then he would've left . . . or would he have been more insistent? . . . Would he have come *looking* for me . . . *knocking* on my door.

At that moment, as I felt Matthew gripping my fingers harder still, I wondered just how much choice I'd had in all of this . . . if I'd ever really had a choice at all . . . if I hadn't come to meet him then would this encounter have taken place in any case?

When I took in Matthew's eyes, did my best to see past all the usual signs of eyes, and look into the person within, I couldn't see anything at all.

Nothing more than another human being.

Living, breathing: yes, all those signs were present.

But I felt nothing.

Nothing attaching him to me, or me to him.

It was then that I knew I should go, that it would be *dishonest* for me to stay any longer. All the correspondence, all those emails we'd flipped back and forth, carefully tiptoeing about our present-day private lives, and remaining pretty much as cool in tone as two acquaintances meeting after a decade-long separation might remain . . . until the text I'd got earlier in the day.

I watched Matthew's Adam's apple bob in his throat, *hard*. And then I saw a slight dampness take over his eyes. "I *can't* go back," he said.

Another Parting

THE FAMILY got up to leave—just as quietly as they'd been through the duration of their stay. No fuss. One of the boys yawning hard, father ruffling his hair as they went. None of them looked at us sat there, the only other people in the café, but why would they have?

There was nothing special to see, just another middle-aged couple having a coffee while waiting between trains.

A *childless* couple.

The bell above the door tinkled the family out of the café, and I noticed the lady at the counter flipping through a magazine neatly concealed behind the till.

I'm not sure what came first. The *tinkle* of the bell or my slithering my fingers out from Matthew's grasp. Bringing my hands back to my chest. Holding them there as if they'd suddenly become very dear to me.

Thinking about it, I quite needed my hands.

They *were* dear to me.

Because without my hands I could not practise my art, and that, after all, was what I loved the most, it was what had cost me what, on less self-esteem-filled days, I might've termed a 'normal' life.

I averted Matthew's gaze. Though there was no clock in sight, I said, "Your train's leaving soon."

Matthew pressed his lips together. His hands now sprawled out on the table between us, apparently unsure where they should lie now that I had withdrawn from them.

I gathered up my handbag, lying beside me, sandwiched between my thigh and the wall of the café. I waited a couple of ticks of my heart and then braved another glance back at Matthew, managed to pin on a smile. "It was nice to meet up," I said. "Maybe another time—another time you're passing through."

His eyes widened. His eyeballs seemed to bulge in their sockets.

I caught myself then.

Told myself that it was time to go.

Now.

I shifted my weight off the plastic bench, felt the sturdy tiled floor beneath the soles of my shoes, and it was then that I knew I could do it. Almost like I'd returned to Earth following a long space flight. Like I could leave now. Do whatever I wanted.

I was *free*.

For the briefest moment I wondered if Matthew would make a scene—if he would snatch hold of my forearm, yank me into him, steal a kiss perhaps, refuse to take 'no' for an answer . . . but he remained still, stunned perhaps, or maybe I'm not giving him enough credit . . . maybe he knew a lost cause when he saw one.

Goodness knows I do . . .

I listened to the hollow echo of the soles of my shoes all around. Bouncing off the walls of the café. Coming on back to me. And seeming to match up with the rhythm of my pulse—every tick of which I could hear bounding in my eardrums.

I glanced briefly to the lady at the counter, managed to summon the merest sliver of a smile for her, and then I bucked on out onto the platform.

All at once I felt that chilly edge to the air—that long-promised September chill, it had arrived, this afternoon it had arrived, while I'd been sitting there, in The Seabrudge Café with Matthew: former lover, fellow veteran of middle-age, and all-over mixed-up man.

As I paced past the window, Matthew stared out from beneath glass.

Only as I caught his eye did I realise that he wasn't looking at me . . . no, he wasn't looking at me at all, he was looking on out to those train tracks, to the tracks which ran in their straight lines, with their sleek, polished-up metal, and which could take him, well, just about anywhere.

Anywhere he wanted to go.

And yet, I think I knew as well as he did, there was only one place for him to go.

He had made that choice.

And it was time for him to stick with it.

Because the two of us had got back in touch, and now we were breaking apart.

Leaving each other forever.

We wouldn't speak again.

BORING PEOPLE
SPECTACULAR CLOTHES

The Incident

I T WAS PRICKLY HOT, and the extra padding at Private
Mumblie's chest really wasn't doing anything to help that.
Although it was the dead of night, Mumblie could still feel the
insufferable desert heat rebounding up at him from his feet.
Whenever he breathed in, he caught grains of sand in his nostrils—
grains of sand which seemed to line the back of his throat like
sandpaper. Mumblie glanced up. He could see them all—*all* of
them—gathered about him. The nine others in his pack. All of
them armed. All of them with their semi-automatic rifles.

Mumblie was no different of course.

The one thing which'd struck him, on the way to the drop, was
the state of their uniforms. Of course there was the extra chest
padding which Mumblie had first believed to be some sort of an
extra precautionary measure—perhaps some new bullet-proofing
technology—but which he had now figured out was merely
cosmetic . . . and, out here in the desert, actually quite deeply
annoying.

But, above all else, it was the *colour* of their uniforms.

How they seemed to be . . . well, there was no other way to
describe it . . . a *patchwork* of just about every other type of camos
that Mumblie had ever laid his eyes on.

How his superiors had ever thought that this sort of a uniform
would help Mumblie, and his companions, get through with this
assassination evaded him. But, just as Mumblie had learned from a
life at war, he wasn't here to ask questions. He was here to stand
and fight. To do what was ordered of him. Just like he would do
tonight. Just like they would do for their *client* tonight. They would
rub out the target, fly home, and get paid.

That was the life's work of the militia man.

Simple.

Clear.

. . . But not necessarily *easy* . . . at least not with these uniforms.

Mumblie turned his attention back to the stone palace ahead of them, and he looked to the banks of sand which built up at its sides. Which layered themselves up against its walls. There was to be nothing subtle about their entrance to the palace . . . which was to say that C4 explosives were involved . . . and although Mumblie wouldn't have thought to speak so much as a word out loud, he was quite aware that the first stage of the operation was particularly delicate, and required, of necessity, that the advanced members of his team—the ones with the explosives—approach without disturbing any of the security systems.

Otherwise, well, they'd all be for it.

Mumblie glanced across his brothers-(and sisters, *siblings* really)-in-arms and waited for the signal. His superior made the gesture and the pair of explosives experts peeled away from the group and, keeping their heads down, gradually made their way towards the palace walls.

Their camos, just like Mumblie had imagined, offered them no protection whatsoever.

As far as Mumblie was concerned, they might as well have both been wearing a pair of fluorescent vests . . . with blinking red lights.

Mumblie had to admit that he wasn't *totally* surprised when he heard the twin *hiss* of sniper rifles, and watched his companions slump down into the midnight sand.

Dead.

And their cover very much blown.

Everything happened quickly from that point on.

Like the rest, Mumblie went to ground. He got a mouthful of sand, and though he tried his best to look up through the glare from the spotlights which sparked up and shone down from the walls of the palace, he found that he couldn't see a damn thing.

One by one, he heard that *hiss* of the sniper shots finding each of his companions who lay in the sand alongside him, until Mumblie caught the awful sensation that he was the last one alive.

Feeling his heart pumping hard—apparently doing its best to break free of his ribcage—and now knowing that he was all alone, Mumblie tried to make a job of lying very still.

Of not moving so much as a hair.

The spotlight swivelled about.

Caught Mumblie a couple of times.

But Mumblie laid himself still.

Forced himself not to move.

And when the spotlight finally clicked off on the palace wall, Mumblie let out a long sigh of relief, and, wriggling on his belly away from his now-dead, mercenary comrades, he wondered just whose bright idea the uniforms had been.

KILL, KILL, KILL, that seemed to be just about the only thing these people wanted to do, and, in all honesty, to Marion, it was positively ghastly.

She approached the dozen or so wax mannequins, located towards the back of the airy, deserted hanger.

The air smelled of oil and actually had a physical effect on her whenever she breathed in. It sent the hair on her arms, and on her legs—this morning there simply *hadn't* been time to shave—standing on end.

She could still taste the plasticky flavour of the capsule of the diet pill she had swallowed not an hour ago: a late breakfast; and she could feel a slightly unwelcome twisting in the pit of her gut. She was a professional, though, so when she came to work, she *came* to work.

Somewhere, off where Marion couldn't see, she could hear something dripping. Perhaps it was connected to the oily smell which cut through the air, and her lungs.

The wax mannequins—or whatever it was that they made them from these days—were all decked out in the half-finished designs from Marion's predecessor.

They were simple designs.

'Forest camos', she supposed they could be termed.

Another mannequin featured camos of icy blues and sharp blacks.

Yet another mannequin hung with sandy yellows, which, and here Marian was fairly certain that she was supposed to catch a clue, were intended for desert 'warfare'.

Marian strutted along the file of mannequins another time, hearing the steady *click-click-click* of her turquoise high heels against the wavered concrete floor of the hanger. She clutched the light, pearl-white, wrap-around robe she wore over the top of her smart trouser suit—also white—and rubbed at her arms in an attempt to guard against the chill.

The draught really *did* creep in about the place.

When she reached the end of the row of mannequins, she stopped dead and then peered back along them. Her eyes prickled across the surface of the mannequins. What she was looking for, she didn't exactly know. All that she could say for certain was that when she saw whatever it was she was looking for then there would be a gentle *ding* within her brain—a little like the miniature bell her grandmother would keep on her bedside table, on a silver tray and beside her crystal medicine receptacles. The bell which her grandmother would use to call for the servants in her dying days. So much grace, so much *glamour* . . . it was enough to send Marian berserk thinking about what her grandmother might make of her now, standing in the middle of this hanger.

Before these mannequins.

Marian tried her best, she really did, but no matter how much she glanced over the mannequins, no matter how she squeezed her eyes shut and peered through their slits, she just couldn't hear that *ding* taking place inside her head. This place, this *hanger*, well, there was only one way to describe it: the place where creativity came to die.

Marian shrugged her shoulders, and primly stepped over to the paint-splattered chair where she had tentatively laid down her fine, white-leather handbag. She unzipped and removed a bottle of perfume from within. A couple of squirts later, and she found herself swimming in the odours of sharp lavender, and a hint of some sort of spice.

It warmed her.

Just a little.

As Marian replaced the perfume bottle within her handbag, zipped it back up again, she could hear footsteps over her shoulder. She turned to look, though she supposed that she knew just who it would be. *Him.* Of course it was *him.*

He wore a sharp, olive-green suit, with a slick, dark, olive-stone brown tie. He had greying hair—how Marian's own might look if she hadn't vigilantly dyed those first greys all those years ago. As he walked the heels of his boots snapped, but, obviously, with a harder, thicker note than Marian's own heels.

Just as he had been when Marian had met him, he wasn't smiling. His features seemed dead set into his skull. Shadows seemed to lurk in his eye sockets. He walked with his arms neatly down at his sides, thumbs always close enough to hook themselves into the pockets of the trousers, but, as Marian knew well, they never would.

That would be disorder, of a kind.

He was no longer wearing the pillar-box cap he had before—one of those *army* hats—and Marian wondered if this might be some sort of a slip of protocol, or perhaps it merely signified that he was becoming more comfortable in her company.

Although Marian wasn't certain where he might've got *that* idea from.

When he reached her, he made all sorts of drama about stopping. Actually *snapping* his heels together smartly. Standing to attention, and, all things considered, making Marian feel extremely uncomfortable.

"At ease, soldier," Marian said, deadpan, but, inside, nursing a gentle smirk.

He peered out from beneath the shadow which lurked over his features. His eyes swivelled about their sockets, neatly, peering along the rows of mannequins. "Are they ready?"

Marian drew in a sharp breath. She had never been much of one for *talking around* the issue, but these soldier types were somewhat ridiculous in her opinion. They certainly cut right to the quick, and manners be damned. "It's going to take *some* time," Marian replied.

"How much time?" he shot back.

Marian laid her tongue down on the base of her mouth. She glanced over his name tag, the one which had been—extremely poorly, and with unflattering, *black* thread—stitched onto the breast pocket of his uniform jacket. *Sergeant Yolahowl.* She wondered if there might be a story behind that name, but quickly decided that, if there indeed was, then he would have no intention of divulging it to her.

"Well," Marian replied, certain to hint at a sigh with her tone, "I would like to have at least another month to speculate before I begin so much as drawing up plans, let alone cutting, or threading, or anything like . . ."

"Twenty-four hours, just like we agreed. That's what you have."

The man—*Sergeant Yolahowl*—stood stock still as he regarded her.

She supposed that, in the soldier brain of his, he was gauging what he perceived to be her weak spots. How, if required, he could make a clean kill. But Marian knew that it wouldn't take much force to *kill* her. She was stick-thin, just as she had always been, and if the soldier man had so much as desired it so, she was certain that he could snap her like a twig.

Marian reluctantly turned her attention back to the mannequins.

The soldier was now pointing at one of the uniforms in particular—the one with the icy blues and coal blacks. "This one," he said. "I need ten copies of *this*."

Marian felt her heart tickle at the base of her throat. She knew that this man was all business, but, really, this was ridiculous.

The soldier met her gaze. His eyes seemed almost black to Marian, though she wasn't certain if it wasn't her imagination playing tricks on her. "Just copy it," the soldier said. "Just like we agreed, okay?" He paused a moment, apparently for emphasis. "Ten of them."

And, with that, a neat turn of heel, the soldier spun off and away from Marian, and marched his way off across the concrete floor—footsteps echoing about—and he disappeared through the darkened doorway at the other end of the hanger.

When she was quite sure he was gone, Marian let out a long-held sigh, and turned back to the mannequins, and then to the transparent, plastic bags which contained her raw materials.

Everything she would need.

The sewing machine just beyond.

What *was* it with some people?

Why did they make such *stringent* demands?

Twenty-Four Hours Before The Incident

MARIAN DECIDED, before she really got to grips with the task at hand, that she needed a good, long doze. The soldiers, when they had brought her here, had shown her to what would be her quarters for the duration of her task. It wasn't much —not much more than a university-style, dormitory bedroom: exposed pipes with chipped, once-white paint, and a steel *cot* with springs that slinked about beneath Marian's weight. There *was* a window, but it was covered in bars, and looked out only onto a sad-looking concrete courtyard.

No plants.

No sky above.

Just *grey.*

Although Marian had only planned on taking one of her world-famous powernaps—in and out in twenty minutes, or, at maximum, half an hour—the powernap of today actually turned into a twelve-hour-long sleepathon.

Perhaps it was the bed, how the springs slinked about and allowed Marian to sink downwards. It certainly wasn't the scratchy, over-washed blankets, or the familiar draught which— just as it did in the hanger—drifted about the place like an unpleasant and unshakable friend. The room, Marian could say for certain, was dark—*extremely* dark—and she wondered if that was another factor at play, allowing her to sleep through the day.

Later, Marian speculated as to whether she might've slept all the way through her deadline if it hadn't been for the percussive *thump-thump* at her chamber door.

When she rose herself out of bed, stepped across the balding carpet, rubbing her eyes with her fists, she felt herself still caught up in dreamland. Her brain still fluttering with subconscious images. Upon opening up the door, though, all those images—swiftly, unceremoniously—flapped away.

She eyed the soldier, standing there, the name tag of his: *Sergeant Yolahowl* . . . the poor stitching was still annoying to her.

The soldier, of course, wished for a progress update—didn't these people *always* want a 'progress' update of some sort?—and Marian informed him, quite honestly, that she continued to allow the ideas to gestate.

That, no matter what he might wish, the soldier couldn't rush art.

This only seemed to bring out the darkened shadows in the soldier's face once more. When he spoke again, his voice was gruff and serious. His jawline suddenly became razor-sharp, and completely set in its position.

If Marian had felt a touch more resilience, she might've asked the soldier to lighten up. But, judging by the way the soldier gripped tight to her arm, twisting it quite hard, Marian decided not to push the issue.

Although Marian knew the route to the hanger perfectly well enough, the soldier led her all the way back there. All the way to her spot before the mannequins. She stood before them, a little stunned, and feeling the soldier's stare pressing down on the backs of her shoulders. She thought, once more, of making some statement about not wanting to rush through this, about how she enjoyed the process of creating clothes more than just about anything in the world . . . but something within her argued against it . . . and she listened to that voice.

Once the soldier was gone, Marian turned her attention back onto the mannequins, and to the uniform which the soldier had instructed her to copy.

There really seemed to be no other option.

MARIAN WOULD'VE LIKED to say that she got on with her work. That she sat down at the sewing machine provided and got busy with the material with which she had been given.

But that wasn't how it happened.

Not at all.

As she felt the gentle, throbbing mechanism of the sewing machine up against her palms, the warmth against her skin, she knew that something just wasn't right. That there was something going on here which she couldn't quite saw the edges off.

This always seemed to happen when some *inconsiderate* thought that the best way to get her up and jumping was to give her a hearty prod in the spine.

As she pulled the third uniform on through the machine, feeling the juddering vibrations passing through her fingertips, she stopped herself all of a sudden.

Struck by a lightning bolt.

By inspiration.

A touch so profound that Marian had to remind herself to breathe.

She gripped on tight to the material, and then swivelled about to the other mannequins.

Her vision was so clear.

So *crisp*.

There was really nothing, of this world, which could stop her once she was in her flow.

And now—undoubtedly—she *was* in her flow.

GLADLY, the soldier left Marian to her task. He apparently saw—quite rightly—that rushing her along was certainly not the way to get the best results. Everybody, all her *employers*, seemed to observe that in the end. Sometimes she did wonder why it took them *so* long.

She pulled through her prototype—all done now—and, when finished, she hung it up on one of the wax mannequins so that she could use it to copy the others across.

Yes, she was sure now that she had found her groove.

That she had, once more, found innovation in even the most barren of places.

ARIAN WORKED QUICKLY. She was well aware of the time now, but, in the same way, it just no longer seemed to be a factor. Once she knew what her work was, what it was that her hands were compelling her to do, she could speed herself up immeasurably. There were no more conscious thoughts driving her forwards. The whole of the design was simply streaming on out *through* her. She didn't need to so much as glance at the proto-type any longer.

That simply wasn't necessary.

She counted out the remaining uniforms—that she needed to do another two, and that she would have plenty of time. *More than enough time*, actually. As it always seemed to pan out in the end.

As Marian closed in on the home stretch, her fingers tugging the material through, and the needle of the sewing machine going *clickety-click*, she almost felt as if somebody might be kneading her brain with their fists, unknotting all the inspiration and pouring it down onto the final design as she brought it out of the imaginary and into the *real*.

And it was only as she let her foot up off the pedal of the sewing machine that she caught the sound of those footsteps once more.

She didn't need to glance about herself this time.

There was no need.

She knew that he was watching her.

That he was gazing along the mannequins.

Taking in her designs.

"What on *Earth* have you done?"

Marian felt herself tense up immediately. She was well-acquainted with the standard reactions of the beleaguered client: that strangest of animals, which, at the bottom of everything else, just didn't seem to *ever* understand what they *really* wanted . . . she had always made it *her* task to bring their brief—kicking and screaming—out of them.

For several moments, she just continued to sit at her sewing machine, feeling the throb of adrenalin seeping through her veins. She still felt like she was on a hot streak, like she could design just about anything if she would only put her mind to it.

She watched on as the soldier entered her vision—his back to her—and she observed as he trudged along the line of mannequins, looking them over with fierce, bulging-wide eyes.

He held his shoulders all hunched, and it seemed that he had gone as rigid as ice.

Marian looked over her shoulder, to the exit out of the hanger, and she wondered if she might be able to make a break for the door, or if the soldier would refuse to allow her to leave. Now that she had—apparently—displeased him.

The soldier reached the end of the row of mannequins, barely shaking his head, apparently from the shock of the whole thing. Finally, he glanced back at her. His eyes remained like a pair of pinpricks in his face. Black dots with no personality, not even communicating the anger that he was surely exhibiting right now. "What have you done?"

Marian felt an overwhelming urge to simply state the obvious, but she held herself back. She glanced along the row of mannequins. Only now did she properly absorb the icy-blue uniforms which she had melded with the sandy yellows, and those khaki greens. What she had created—she was sure—was nothing short of utterly unique design.

And yet, her client was displeased.

The soldier shook his head now, and Marian noted how his cheeks coloured slightly. She supposed this was how he would get with his inferiors, that he would turn that ire of his onto them with all the efficiency of the bendy neck of a high-wattage desk lamp.

"The brief," he said, "was *very* clear." He gestured to the uniforms: all of the ones which the soldier had commissioned Marian to cobble together. "Just to *copy* what we already had. Was that not clear enough for you?"

Marian shrugged her shoulders, gave a vague grin.

This only seemed to infuriate the soldier all the more.

"What you've done," the soldier said, shaking his head, "it's just . . . I can't . . . how did you . . ."

But he seemed lost for words. He wasn't making a jot of sense.

Marian knew that it was moments like these when she needed to shift herself onto her feet. It was always better for her to be standing . . . *just in case.*

The soldier turned back to the uniforms, looked them over, his eyes skittering about their sockets. "I can't . . . I mean, we *can't* . . . can't even just use distinct uniforms, we'll have to . . . need to . . ."

It was here that Marian felt another overwhelming urge, but, this time, it wasn't one which involved fleeing the scene just as quickly as her toothpick legs could carry her. No, that wouldn't make a plan at all. She was sure that, just like any self-respecting army man, this soldier right here would be quite capable of running her down.

She sidled up to the army man, and she laid her arm on his shoulder. Gave his shoulder a gentle squeeze. Maybe she expected the soldier to snap, to spin around and blaze a whole host of obscenities at her. But he didn't move. He stood stock still, apparently, now, unmoved by anything at all.

"It'll be okay," Marian said. "Just give them a go, huh?"

The soldier continued to stare on at the mannequins, and the designs which Marian had so lovingly cobbled together from the *so few* materials she had had to work with.

And then, feeling that now was her moment to give the soldier some alone time, she removed her hand from his shoulder, and stepped away from him. Padded her way across the concrete floor of the hanger, leaving him behind.

He, of course, did nothing to stop her.

He had been the one who had hired her.

And, as Marian swept on out through the 'top-secret' bunker, and into the beaming, morning sunlight where the helicopter which'd brought her here awaited, she speculated at how her life had turned out.

How, more and more these days, she was having to get used to dealing with these boring people who just didn't understand spectacular clothes.

AUTHOR'S NOTE

Thank you for taking the time to read one of my books. If you would like to hear about my latest releases you can sign up for my newsletter here: www.tjbainz.com

Thanks for reading!

TJ Bainz

The Mind's Aspiration
A Short Story Collection

www.ingramcontent.com/pod-product-compliance
Lightning Source LLC
Chambersburg PA
CBHW020947260626
47169CB00006B/1869